"Whew," Sarah said, drawing out the chair opposite Heath's.

Her pale complexion was flushed and the afternoon's heat had dampened the tendrils hugging the nape of her neck where she'd pulled back her hair. "That was tough," she added.

"I'd have thought you'd be an old pro at a simple lunch," Heath said.

"Oh, sure," she replied. "I just didn't get much rest last night. But now that my right-hand person has finally gotten here, I've got time for a breather."

After a few moments of awkward silence, he leaned forward, toying with his blue napkin. "Not that it's my business, but why'd you get a lousy night's rest?"

"Why do you care?"

"No reason," he said. "Sorry I asked. I was just trying to make small talk, but maybe my question came out as invasive."

"No," she said, staring at Heath straight on, and then sighing. "Truthfully, I didn't get a wink of sleep last night for a fairly simple reason—you."

Dear Reader,

On the topic of twins, seeing as how I have a set of my own, I'm a bit biased. I *love* twin stories, which is what makes Heath and Sarah's tale extra dear to my heart.

I suppose my fascination with twins started with Disney's *The Parent Trap* (both the Hayley Mills and Lindsay Lohan versions). The whole concept of being able to exchange lives with someone is very intriguing! Alas, unless Mom and Dad are hiding a deep family secret, I'll never get to discover how much fun this could actually be. And seeing as I was blessed with boy/girl twins, there won't be any switcheroos going on at our house. Meaning my only shot for twin mayhem is in the pages of my books.

I so hope you'll enjoy taking Heath and Sarah's wild ride with me as they both try to convincingly fill their twins' shoes—usually failing miserably in every area but love!

Best,

Laura Marie ;-)

The Right Twin
LAURA MARIE ALTOM

HARLEQUIN®

TORONTO • NEW YORK • LONDON
AMSTERDAM • PARIS • SYDNEY • HAMBURG
STOCKHOLM • ATHENS • TOKYO • MILAN • MADRID
PRAGUE • WARSAW • BUDAPEST • AUCKLAND

ISBN-13: 978-0-373-75164-8
ISBN-10:   0-373-75164-8

THE RIGHT TWIN

www.eHarlequin.com

Printed in U.S.A.

Trust me, I do. Otherwise you'd have never in a million, trillion years entrusted me with this pile of wood and bricks that you've made your life's work." Releasing her hands from Sadie's in order to raise her right one, Sarah added, "That's why, as my most solemn oath on the Royal Order of Cookie Thieves, I hereby promise to make each of your guests this weekend fall wholly, completely and madly in love with your inn and also you."

Sadie's throat tightened at the reference to the to secret club she and her twin had formed back in fourth grade for the purpose of launching stealth missions to nab the heavenly cookies their mother baked for wealthy St. Louis clients. Whereas Sadie had taken after their mother, Sarah had chosen their father to look up to and was now climbing a corporate ladder instead.

"Well…" Sadie said, biting her lower lip. "I very much want everyone to adore the inn, but they don't particularly even need to like me—just see that I run a tight ship. And you know there's still a chance the *Zodor's* reviewer could show. Otherwise I wouldn't have needed to involve you. But if by chance he or she does make an appearance and I'm not here…"

"Gotcha," her twin said, executing a saucy salute.

For the umpteenth time since Sadie had formed the plan that would—if all went well—allow her to be in two places at once, she actually dared a normal breath.

For nearly two years now, she'd been engaged to Trevor.

The man was tall, dark, handsome and charming and yet he seemed utterly incapable of setting a wedding date.

Which was why, when he'd accused *her* of being responsible for the holdup on their trip down the aisle, she'd agreed to give up minding her inn this weekend and accompany him to his sister's wedding in Tulsa in exchange for his promise to set a wedding date of their own. Sadie had to take the chance.

In Trevor she would have the perfect husband, as well as a superb host for her guests. Gorgeous, easy to talk to and successful in his own right, Trevor was a great catch. As much as she loved her inn, she loved Trevor even more. Otherwise she'd have never asked her twin to agree to such a drastic stunt.

For most inns—most innkeepers—it wouldn't matter if they took time off even while they were being reviewed. But Sadie had worked so hard to get where she was and she took great pride in personally greeting each guest.

Granted, they probably didn't care quite so much if they met her, but she did.

On each bit of advertising was a likeness of Sadie, promising guests that she personally guaranteed they'd enjoy their stay or she'd gladly refund their money. And now, with the chance of being reviewed by a national publication in the wind, there was even more than usual at stake.

Bottom line, she wouldn't have a bit of fun with Trevor if she spent her time worrying over whether or not her inn's reputation was suffering due to someone feeling they hadn't received top-notch personal service.

As for Sarah successfully replacing her, it was Sadie's sincerest hope that she'd arranged enough help so that all her twin would have to do was stand around, smile and be charming.

"Trust me," Sarah said. "Before the weekend's over, you and Trevor will be more in love than ever. While I'm stuck here, coated in flour and slaving away."

Seeing past her sister's teasing grin to the sincerity that shimmered in her mossy-green eyes, Sadie swallowed hard.

Yes, it was sappy and stupid and sentimental, but the inn was like a child to her. A demanding spoiled child that she knew she'd have to relax her grip on one day. Until that day, however, she would be enormously grateful to her twin. "Have I mentioned lately how much I love you?"

"Nope. American Express will do nicely, though, to get your point across."

"I'm serious," Sadie said, giving her sister a gentle swat. "Thank you. Nobody but you could've ever pulled this off."

"Thank *you*," Sarah said.

"For what?"

"Trusting me. I promise I won't let you down. This weekend will be perfect."

With a lifetime of reading each other, they rose at precisely the same time, wrapping each other in teary hugs.

"For the record," Sarah added, "Italian meringue is made by whipping a boiling syrup into the egg whites."

And with that remark from her sister, Sadie finally relaxed. Her inn would be in excellent hands. As for the odds of a reviewer showing up? Nonexistent.

Chapter One

"Help!"

Heath Brown—identical twin to Hale Brown, who was the renowned food critic for *Zodor's International Country Inn Review Guide*—rushed across Blueberry Inn's reception area to aid a wobbling stack of towels that happened to have great legs. Dropping his black weekender on the floor, Heath grabbed the bulk of the folded laundry, in the process revealing a lovely surprise.

"Thanks, Kim." The bearer of towels had been grinning, but now she frowned. "Er, you're not Kim. Sorry."

"No need for apologies," Heath said. "We can all find ourselves in a laundry crisis now and then." He repositioned his pile. "Where do you want these?"

"Oh…" Laughing, the woman lurched into action, setting her stack on top of an intricately carved walnut reception desk, then turning to face him again. "Here will be fine."

Heath cozied his stack alongside hers.

"Thanks. I hadn't realized I'd grabbed quite so much and I thought that Kim—the housekeeper—was right behind me."

"Again, not a problem."

"Now, how can I help you?"

"I just need to check in."

"Then you're in the right place." Long, buttery hair eased over her shoulders, and her friendly smile crinkled the corners of her eyes. Intriguing eyes. Olive-green. As easy to lose himself in as one of the martinis Heath favored after a long day's work. "Welcome to Blueberry Inn. I'm the owner, Sadie Connelly." She held out her hand for him to shake. Which he did. And when the brief touch struck him as not too hard and not too soft but oddly just right, he was almost reluctant to let her go. Ludicrous in light of what he'd been through with Tess just six months earlier.

"Nice to meet you. I'm Shane Peters." *But for only one weekend.* "I should, uh, have a reservation."

"I know." She winked and then rounded the desk's nearest corner. "I recognize the name—only, isn't your reservation for two?"

Heath's heart lurched. To avoid suspicion, Hale always attached a fictional girlfriend to his fictional name. But for the life of him, Heath couldn't recall the backstory Hale had told him to deliver to explain what had happened to the poor girl. "Um, yes, well, at the last minute *Susie* had something come up."

"I'm sorry," Sadie responded. "Hopefully even without her you'll still manage to grab plenty of R & R."

"That'd be great," Heath replied. After meeting his

hot innkeeper, he now gave the weekend at least a chance of being more entertaining than the two-day nap he'd imagined it would be.

"If you'll give me a sec, I'll find the—here it is." She brandished a navy leather volume about the size of a high school yearbook. Embossed in elegant silver script across the front was *Blueberry Inn*.

"Now, if I could just find a pen…"

"Got one," Heath said, reaching into the pocket of the sports jacket his brother had insisted he wear over his usual casual fare of jeans and a T-shirt. He handed over the pen, in the process, inadvertently brushing his fingers against Sadie's. Instant chemistry tightened his stomach.

"Thanks," his hostess said, her shaky grin somehow leaving him with the impression that all wasn't quite right. Had she felt the same electricity? "I don't know what's wrong with me today." She tapped herself on the forehead. "I can't seem to pull it together—I haven't even had time to dress myself properly." She gestured to her frayed cutoffs and snug pink tee. She looked proper enough to Heath.

"Don't sweat it," he said, charmed by the warmth of her smile and her ability to laugh at herself. "I've had a few of those days myself." Which was part of the reason he'd agreed to this stunt with his twin. Sure, there'd be some work involved in reviewing the inn, but mostly it offered Heath the chance for a much-needed break.

"Thanks for understanding," she said, rifling through the desk drawers. Registration forms? "I know they're here somewhere," Sadie murmured to herself with a cute furrowing of her eyebrows.

Time for a reality check: the fact that Heath had even noticed her eyebrows, on top of her many other charms, could cause him nothing but trouble.

Heath was at Blueberry Inn for only one reason, and that was to bail his brother out of a jam. He owed his twin for the way Hale had ultimately opened his eyes to Tess's deception. The least he could do was cover while Hale was off chasing his secret career dream of becoming a champion drag racer. Sure, most guys would just take time off work to pursue their dreams, but Hale's boss was a hard-nosed taskmaster. He didn't permit moonlighting, and when he made an unusual assignment such as this one—for Hale to go into an establishment ASAP—he meant business. Apparently that same boss's wife—also the money behind the publication—had been so enchanted with the inn during a recent stay that she wanted it featured in a special pullout section on entrepreneurial women in the next edition. According to Hale, the inn's perfection made the awarding of a top rating of five silver spoons a mere formality.

All of which was well and good for Heath's brother to say, but insofar as Tess had taught Heath to despise liars, he hated the thought that his every word and action—even his name—over the long weekend would have to be false. Still, it couldn't be helped.

Besides which, Heath's falsehoods wouldn't harm Sadie Connelly. Unlike Tess's lies, which had cost him and his company millions through corporate espionage. If Sadie Connelly was even half as talented in the kitchen as his brother claimed, she had nothing to sweat.

As much as possible, Heath would relax and be

himself, relishing the rare time away from what his
brother referred to as his obsession of a career—video
game designing. Heath would be the first to admit he'd
put in hellacious hours of late, but what else did he
have to do?

It wasn't as if he had anyone waiting for him at home.
He didn't even have a pet. Just himself. And another in
a long line of lonely nights, a bowl of ramen noodles and
whatever happened to be on ESPN.

Boo hoo. Cry me a river.

After what Tess had put him through, why would
he even want more? The question was logical
enough. Trouble was, he very much wanted more.
He wanted a wife and kids and a family to call his
own so badly that the yearning brought on an embarrassing ache.

What was wrong with him?

As a relatively good-looking and successful
bachelor, he should've been having the time of his
life. Not moping about what might have been. Certainly not about whether or not he'd ever find a
woman—or love—again. But for as long as he could
remember, his mom had always called him her sensitive son.

Clear in his mind was the memory of riding his
bike one flawless July afternoon when he'd been nine.
Not a breath of wind, locusts troubling dusty weeds on
either side of the dirt road and their monotonous hum.
Riding along, counting the licks on a cherry Tootsie
Pop, he'd come upon a bird, fluttering on the powdery
shoulder. Pulling alongside to investigate, he'd seen
that the small brownish-gray bird wasn't indulging in

a dust bath but was struggling at a far more solemn task. Its mate had been crushed.

The little bird tried and tried to wake its companion, thrusting its beak under a broken wing, urging the female to fly.

Fast as he could, Heath rode home to get his mother. She'd climbed on her own bike and dutifully followed. But now, as an adult, Heath knew there was nothing she could have done.

By the time they'd returned, the male had exhausted himself and he sat alongside his mate shuddering with each breath.

Heath had started to cry, begging his mom to do something, and she'd held him close, smoothing his hair and telling him love wasn't easy. She'd promised him that one day, like the bird, he'd find a special girl, and when he married her, there'd be no guaranteeing forever. He'd just have to savor each day for the jewel it was.

In meeting Tess, Heath had thought he'd found his jewel, only to discover, instead, cold, unyielding stone. Hardening his jaw, he glanced over his shoulder to an eight-paned window. He hated to think that the woman still held emotional power in his life.

"Aha!" The innkeeper had found a stack of forms and now she took one from the top, shoving the rest behind the counter. "Once you fill this out, I'll take you to your room."

Heath made quick work of his assignment, glad for the distraction from memories he'd just as soon forget.

When he'd finished, Sadie retrieved a brass key ring with the number nine engraved on it, then stepped from behind the desk. "Want me to get that?" She nodded toward his bag.

"No, thanks." A chivalrous streak had him reaching for it himself.

"Okay, then," she said, making a sweeping gesture toward the stairs. "Follow me and we'll get you squared away so you can relax before lunch."

Considering the caliber of the present view, Heath was pleased to oblige. The woman his brother had described as one of the premier hostesses in the country, well-rounded in all types of cooking and the genteel manners of the sort to instantly put the most disgruntled guest at ease, was also a serious looker. At least five-ten with an abundance of curves.

Heath had been so busy admiring her endless legs that it had barely registered how tough a time she'd had checking him in. Not that it mattered—it just seemed odd.

Up curved stairs and then down a wide hall lined with antique side tables and chairs and bucolic landscapes. His guide stopped before a door, easing the key into the lock.

"Here you go," she said, turning the latch and door, then stepping back with a flourish. "This is the Mark Twain Suite and features whitewashed walls in honor of Huck Finn and memorabilia of the author's life. One of our most prized acquisitions is this letter to his daughter, Clara, written in 1904."

"Um, thanks," Heath said. Not that he wasn't impressed with the room's overall ambience, but Sadie's delivery style sounded rushed—as if she'd been up all night memorizing the description. "How long have you been running this place?"

ABOUT THE AUTHOR

After college (Go Hogs!), bestselling, award-winning author Laura Marie Altom did a brief stint as an interior designer before becoming a stay-at-home mom to boy/girl twins. Always an avid romance reader, she knew it was time to try her hand at writing when she found herself replotting the afternoon soaps.

When not immersed in her next story, Laura enjoys an almost glamorous lifestyle of zipping around in a convertible while trying to keep her dog from leaping out, and constantly striving to reach the bottom of the laundry basket—a feat she may never accomplish! For real fun, Laura is content to read, do needlepoint and cuddle with her kids and handsome hubby.

Laura loves hearing from readers at either P.O. Box 2074, Tulsa, OK 74101, or e-mail: BaliPalm@aol.com. Love lounging on the beach while winning fun stuff? Check out www.lauramariealtom.com.

Books by Laura Marie Altom

HARLEQUIN AMERICAN ROMANCE

1028—BABIES AND BADGES
1043—SANTA BABY
1074—TEMPORARY DAD
1086—SAVING JOE*
1099—MARRYING THE MARSHAL*
1110—HIS BABY BONUS*
1123—TO CATCH A HUSBAND*
1132—DADDY DAYCARE
1147—HER MILITARY MAN

*U.S. Marshals

For my precious Hannah—
you asked for it, you got it!

P.S. Buddy Love, you get the next one!

Prologue

"Pop quiz. What's the difference between Italian meringue and standard?" When Sadie Connelly's sister Sarah's only reply was a deer-in-the-headlights stare, her stomach fell more sharply than a jostled soufflé. "Sweetie," she said with a moan, "this is elementary stuff. If we're to have a chance at pulling this off, you've got to pay attention."

"I am," her twin said, fidgeting in her seat in the Blueberry Inn's sumptuous dining room. A gleaming maple floor inlaid with cherry was softened in spots by colorful Persian rugs. Walls covered in a navy-and-white toile were accented by Sadie's extensive collection of Blue Willow china and her nineteenth-century pastoral prints. Tall windows draped in navy velvet brought in the midspring morning sun and the heady scents of a freshly watered garden that was already riotously in bloom. In the distance, Blue Lake shimmered with the breeze.

All her life Sadie had dreamed of running such a

fabulous inn. Maybe the desire had arisen from watching too much of that old nighttime TV soap *Hotel,* but years later, when their grandmother died and left Sadie the means to not just work in a country inn but actually own one, she'd jumped at the chance.

And jumped and jumped to restore the faded Queen Anne property to its former glory. Five long years later, sweat equity had turned the inn, an hour south of St. Louis, into the ultimate in refined elegance.

"All right then," Sadie said, not sure her sister Sarah realized the gravity of this situation. "If you truly have been paying attention, name it."

"What?"

"The *difference.*"

"In what?"

"Meringue," Sadie said, slapping her palm on the linen tablecloth. "Meringue, meringue, mer—"

"Chill," Sarah interjected. "Seriously. Your second-in-command will soon be here, hovering over me with her beady eyes."

"Helga isn't the least bit 'beady,' in fact, she—"

"Relax. When it comes to supervising me in your sainted kitchen, she's not only beady-eyed, but she's got that creepy stare that she does. As an added bonus, she'll keep all of your other worker bees in line, too. And on top of that, you've laid in enough frozen dinners and pastries to feed ten times the amount of guests you're expecting."

"Yes, but…"

Sadie's twin sighed, then reached for her hands, giving her icy fingers a reassuring squeeze. "I know how much this weekend with Trevor means to you.

"Five years." She flashed him a smile. "This inn's my pride and joy."

He nodded, unsure of what to say. Something about her mannerisms struck him as off—especially for someone who'd been following the same routine for so long. But then, lord knew he'd had a few off days himself at the height of his Tess fiasco. Maybe Sadie had just argued with a member of her staff? The other half of her towel team?

"Anyway," she said with an awkward flap of her hands, "lunch will be served in the dining room at one. I hope you enjoy your stay."

"Thanks. I'm sure I will."

"And don't hesitate to tell me or one of the staff if you need more towels or a snack—or whatever." She flashed another of her cute toothy grins and then she was off, shutting the door behind her.

IN THE HALL, RESTING her shoulders against Shane Peters's door, tightly shutting her eyes, Sarah finally exhaled. What a mess that had been. She'd expected him to arrive with a girlfriend in tow. Sadie had warned her to be on the lookout for single guests who could possibly be from *Zodor's,* but the way Shane had leaped to her aid with the towels hardly made him seem the snooty reviewer type. Besides which, he'd planned to arrive with a weekend date. It would hardly be professional for a reviewer to bring a date, now would it?

Pulling herself together, she hustled down the hall to the back stairs. In Sadie's room, as Sarah should have done an hour earlier, Sarah exchanged her comfy clothes for sharply creased khakis and a white blouse. The bulk of the inn's guests would be arriving within the hour, and now that she'd worked out the registration process with gorgeous Mr. Peters, she hoped that from here on out her check-in duties would be smooth as silk.

Sarah added a string of her sister's pearls and matching earrings to her ensemble, then swirled her hair into a French twist. With a spritz of a light floral scent and fresh lip gloss, she was good to go.

Mmm…Mr. Peters. Truth be told, her quick change had more to do with that one new guest than with the other anticipated arrivals. Had she only imagined the electricity between them when they'd touched? It had been so sweet of him coming to her rescue in the lobby. Then he'd been so patient while she'd fumbled for the registration forms.

All in all, he seemed like a nice guy—a drastic departure from Greg. It was even a relief that her attraction meter still worked.

Her cell chirped out the *Gilligan's Island* theme song.

She glanced at the caller ID, only to roll her eyes. "Hey, sis. What's up?"

"Not much. Just checking in. Have any of our couples arrived?"

"Half of one."

"What do you mean *half*?"

"On Peters-plus-guest, the guest backed out on him."

"You don't think he could be the reviewer, do you? Pulling something sneaky?"

"Not a chance. Too good-looking, laid-back and not at all uptight."

"Sarah…" her sister warned, her voice nearly a growl.

"What?"

"Just in case…don't even think about starting something with him."

"Good grief. I'm barely over Greg. What makes you think I'm anywhere near ready to jump in the dating pool again?"

"I don't know. Something in your tone of voice."

"My tone?" Sarah laughed.

"It's me, remember? I have a sixth sense about you and men."

"Right. Like Helga claims to have her all-seeing man eye?"

"That's exactly right. Don't knock it. And even if he is hot, you won't have time for romance. And another thing—I don't want anyone thinking I'm fraternizing with the guests. Or, for that matter, cheating on Trevor."

Sarah sighed. "Again, after the head trip Greg pulled on me, I'm in no shape to think about any guy. Plus, I only said the guy was hot. Not that I'm going to marry him and have his babies."

"There's no need to get snippy. I have a reputation to uphold."

"Which *you* will. Trust me, okay?"

After a few beats of silence, Sarah's twin said, "I'll think about it."

TWO HOURS LATER, Sarah wished she were anywhere other than immersed in serving the inn's hectic lunch. Backing against the kitchen's pass-through door, Sarah took a deep breath, willing her pulse to slow as she pasted on one of her sister's trademark serene smiles. One thing that helped her relax, at least partially, was that the sun-flooded dining room was a world away from the frenzied pace of the kitchen.

She took a deep breath and then headed for the man who had already become her least favorite guest.

"About time," Mr. Standridge said. With his double chin, permed suspiciously black hair and small gold hoop earring, Sarah imagined the portly man as a retired pirate. Only that picture was somewhat skewed by the fact that Mrs. Standridge's loose white bun made her a dead ringer for Mrs. Claus. Although, Sarah thought as she set two plates of roast beef in front of them, stranger things could happen than Mrs. Claus and Blackbeard having a scandalous affair at her sister's inn.

Not trying too terribly hard to hide her grin, she looked up to find herself face-to-face with Shane Peters. His angular features sported a half day's stubble, and his smiling eyes were as blue as the berries on her sister's stationery logo. Quite simply, the man was breathtaking. And the fact that she'd even noticed was a sure sign that, yes, stranger things than a pirate Mrs. Claus scandal could happen!

Mr. Standridge cleared his throat. "Freshly cracked pepper, please."

"And I still haven't gotten my Chablis," Mrs. Standridge complained.

"Need more of my help?" Shane asked with a teasing grin, helping himself to the best seat in the room beside open French doors.

"I'm thinking maybe so," she said with a discreet wink that she hadn't intended on being flirty.

"Ma'am?" Mr. Standridge glowered.

"I would really like more tea," Mrs. Helsing said with a wag of her empty glass. As robust as the Standridges were, the Helsings were stick-thin and white. Pasty yet slick. Complexions like Crisco.

"And when you get a chance," Mr. Helsing said, "could I please get a new fork? The tines on this one are smudged."

"Certainly, sir. Right away."

"I hate to be contrary," the woman who'd introduced herself as "the widow" Naomie Young said in a cottony tone that matched her fragile frame and pale blue eyes, "but I prefer white bread to pumpernickel."

"Yes, ma'am. I'll have fresh white bread right out."

Sarah managed a feeble smile, took one last intrigued glance at Shane, then worked up a sweat attempting to fulfill her guests' never-ending requests. If only the two of them had met under other circumstances.

"THAT WAS DELICIOUS," Heath said, toward the meal's end, to the couple he'd heard addressed as the Standridges. He introduced himself as his brother had instructed, being careful to maintain a chatty, conversational tone and not tipping off anyone as to the true nature of his visit. "So far, what do you think of the inn?" he asked.

"The decor's lovely," Mrs. Standridge offered, glancing over her shoulder before speaking again. Checking to see if Sadie was out of the room? "But the food…" She blanched.

"You didn't care for it?" Heath asked, more than a little surprised, since he'd enjoyed his roast beef, mashed potatoes and gravy.

"It was tasty enough," the woman said, "but a smidge heavy for my tastes. Reminiscent of a high-end TV dinner."

"Not that we were eavesdropping," the female half of the Helsing couple said, "but I booked this weekend because of fantastic recommendations from several of our friends. I enjoyed the meal, but the service seemed lackluster, if not altogether slow."

Mr. Helsing nodded. "There were several times when my iced-tea glass was empty, and I had to wait a full three minutes or more for a refill."

The horror.

Why, Heath couldn't say, but as he made careful mental notes of a litany of bogus halfhearted complaints, he felt sorry for Sadie. According to his brother, the Blueberry Inn was one of the best-kept secrets in the Midwest—which was why the *Zodor's* editor in chief was so hot to get the scoop.

Keeping that in mind—and registering the fact that he'd completely enjoyed his own lunch—Heath took his fellow diners' complaints with a grain of salt. By the time the disgruntled bunch had wandered off to their rooms or the garden for reading or an afternoon nap, he'd pretty much decided that if dinner was as tasty as lunch, he'd simply strike the petty negativity from his files.

Experience had taught him that building your own business was tough. Other than the time it had taken Sadie to get him registered and that mile-a-minute room description, he hadn't noticed anything even remotely remiss. And so what if she had ever so slightly fudged those couple of tasks? Just as he'd been burned by the discovery that it was his latest game design that Tess had really lusted after, maybe there was some sort of behind-the-scenes situation going on with Sadie. Something she had too much class to let him or any of her other guests see.

He'd just discreetly tucked his notepad into his jacket pocket when the woman at the center of his thoughts entered the dining room. The fact that the mere sight of her produced a pleasurable jolt set him on edge. The last time he'd felt an instant attraction had been with Tess.

"Whew," Sarah said, drawing out the chair opposite Heath's. Her pale complexion was flushed, and the afternoon's heat dampened the tendrils that hugged the nape of her neck where she'd pulled back her hair. Would her skin taste salty? That tempting spot on her neck? As if it were possible to shake the thought from his mind, Heath shook his head, but the motion didn't help. Big surprise. "That was tough."

"I'd have thought you'd be an old pro at a simple lunch."

"Oh, sure," she said. "I just didn't get much rest last night. But now that my right-hand person has finally fixed her car's flat, I've got time for a breather."

"Congratulations," he said.

"Thanks."

After a few moments' awkward silence, he leaned forward, toying with his blue napkin. "Not that it's my business, but why?"

"Why what? Why was Helga's tire flat?"

"No," he said with a laugh. "Why'd you get a lousy night's rest?"

"Oh, *that*." She leaned back in her chair.

Had his question been too forward? Probably. Regardless, Heath forged ahead. "Simple enough question."

"W-why do you care?"

Would Heath's brother care?

Who could explain it, but for whatever odd reason, Heath felt a compelling urge to know something more about what made the lovely innkeeper tick. From the time they'd met until now, her appearance had gone from frazzled to casual grace. Which image was the real Sadie? Over the course of the weekend, would he get the chance to learn the answer? With elegant fingers, she traced the floral-patterned white-on-white tablecloth.

"No reason," he said, covering for himself when it seemed she preferred to avoid the topic. "Sorry I asked. I was just trying to make small talk, but maybe my question came out as invasive."

"No," she said, staring at Heath straight on and then sighing. "Truthfully, I didn't get a wink of sleep last night for a fairly simple reason. You."

Chapter Two

"Me?" Eyebrows raised, Heath said, "I'd like to be flattered, but judging by your pained expression, it wasn't my devastating good looks that kept you up."

Sarah laughed. "Not specifically you, per se, but folks like you. Guests."

"Why? I mean, this is your livelihood. Has been for, what, five years you said?"

She nodded, leaning forward with her elbows on the table. "But I'll let you in on a little secret." One that Sadie had shared with her not too long ago. "The more I'm in the business, the more it seems my guests are getting harder to spoil. To well and truly please. The big chains have phenomenal employee bases, while I'm just me—and a few trusted employees who've become dear friends."

"Friends who help fend off *me?* The *enemy?*" He laughed again, clearly poking fun at himself.

Was it wrong to be affected by the rich, mellow voice of the guy that your sister had specifically told you was hands-off? Probably, but Shane Peters's laughter struck Sarah as delicious. Tempting. Like a superrich dessert you knew you shouldn't have but were hard-pressed to resist. Alas, because of her deep sense of respect for Sadie, she would resist. Not only because the man was off-limits for the sake of her sister, but because of the pain she still felt from her involvement with Greg.

She wasn't ready to open herself up to another man.

"You're hardly the enemy," Sarah said. "It's just that…I've worked hard for this." She gestured toward the opulence of the inn's dining room. Antique tables, linens and china. Blue-and-white-toile walls and ornate moldings. Gentle sun slanting through open French doors, leading to a dreamy garden. A hundred varieties of blooms that Sarah couldn't begin to name. Sweet and lovely, humming with butterflies and bees. Beyond that, a lake so crystalline and blue and in perfect harmony with the wedding cake of a house on its shore that her sister had said she'd shed a few tears the first time she'd seen it. And all of this—every last bit—was in Sarah's hands right now.

Granted, her sister was arguably deranged when it came to her love for the place, but Sarah knew that Sadie had worked hard to achieve all this, and out of love and respect for her twin, Sarah intended to maintain her sister's standards. Even if the dreaded reviewer never showed.

"Sometimes," Sarah said, again sharing more of Sadie than herself, "I want perfection so much, that I…" She shook her head. "Sorry. I'm just rambling on about nothing, when you're here to relax and not listen to me whine."

Shane flashed her a smile of such warm concern

Sarah knew in a heartbeat he was sincere. And then she swallowed a sour taste in her mouth over the notion that at the moment she was anything but sincere.

Oh, she was sincere in terms of being nervous. But it pained her to think that this compassionate man was actually sympathizing with her over a lie.

"Relax," he said. "From all I've heard, this place is a little slice of heaven, right here in your corner of Missouri. And, you know, maybe this bout of nerves is your body's way of telling you you've been working too hard. Maybe if you'd try stealing a few minutes for yourself here and there, you'd be back to business as usual."

Great theory. Trouble was *business as usual* for Sarah consisted of working from eight to six at the accounting firm of Geoffrey, Deloite & Bartholomew. It was Sarah's dream to one day have her name added to the list of partners. Numbers were her game, whereas for as long as she could remember, Sadie had been into the whole hearth-and-home thing.

Like her father, Sarah had toyed with the idea of going into physics, but seeing how she also had a thing for nice shoes and expensive handbags, she'd opted for accounting over science. Where Shane had been telling "Sadie" to relax, the reality was that the real Sadie was thrilled with her life. It was Sarah who needed rest and relaxation to put things into perspective. What had happened with Greg had shaken her to the core, had made her distrust not only other people but herself.

"What's the matter?" her new friend asked in a light tone. "My pep talk was supposed to bring back your smile—not make you scowl."

"Sorry," she said with a hesitant laugh. "Promise, I'll try to do more guffawing."

"You'd better," Heath teased. "Otherwise I just may remind you of that full-satisfaction clause in your ads. You know, the one that promises guests will be one hundred percent thrilled with their stay or you'll give them a full refund?"

Groaning, Sarah said, "I know the one." That silly clause was another reason that she was having to step in for her sister. God forbid any guest should have a complaint and not be able to deliver it to the inn's owner herself. "Dumbest thing I ever did, making that promise."

"Oh, I don't know…" Heath toyed with a silver-and-crystal saltshaker. "That phrase strikes me as pretty sexy. The confidence behind your statement shows you to be a powerful woman. Wholly in control."

Ha! Her sister was all that.

Sarah, however, had never felt more out of control.

Pulse racing, mouth dry, head spinning—she had serious problems. Not the least of which was that just this once she wanted to feel that way again. Powerful and in control. She used to, but then Greg had gone and done a number on her head. Lying about so many things that her whole life had been turned upside down. Leading her to this moment, when here she sat with an amazing guy and was actually afraid to like him!

Beyond the primary fact that Sadie would disapprove, Sarah knew she wasn't ready for even casual flirtation, let alone anything more serious. Like the kind of deep-seated emotions called for in mutual trust.

"Sadie?" he prompted. "You're scowling again."

"Yes, I am," she said, "and it's getting tiresome."

Determined to cast aside doubt and worry for the few remaining minutes she had before she needed to help her sister's crew get started on dinner, Sarah said to her guest, "Let's change the topic to something more light-hearted. Like you telling me what you do for fun?"

Glancing out at the garden, then looking up at the ceiling and ultimately giving her a shrug, he said, "Work keeps me busy."

"Oh, come on," she teased. "Don't tell me you're one of those guys for whom work is his entire life. What's your passion? What do you do for a living that's so all-consuming?"

"I'm a computer game designer. Ever heard of Seether?"

"Heck, yeah. That's only like *PC Gaming*'s game of the year. You designed that?"

"You don't have to sound so shocked."

"I'm not, it's just that I'm a huge fan. That's one of the best games ever."

"And you've had time to play…when?"

"*Very* rarely," Sarah quickly volleyed, remembering that she was temporarily her sister, who had never in her life played a computer game other than solitaire. "But when I have, those three-headed nanobeasts are hell. Meeting the guy who actually dreamed them up is a thrill."

"Wow, thanks," he said, his gaze darting away, as if her praise embarrassed him. "Talking to you could be seriously good for my ego."

"With your talent, I wouldn't think you'd need an ego boost."

Grinning and shaking his head, he admitted,

"That used to be the case, but then, I met up with a woman who—"

"Sadie, hon," Helga called through the kitchen door. "When you get a sec, I need your help with the dinner menu."

Sarah groaned. "Be right there!" Why did Helga the Horrible need her right now? Just when the conversation had taken such an interesting turn? "Sorry. If you wouldn't mind, I'd love to continue our chat later."

"Sure," he said, dazzling her with his smile. "Just so happens I'll be around till Sunday."

"WHAT?" HEATH BARKED into his cell upon recognizing the caller ID. He was intent on finishing his run around the inn's lake. Even more, he was intent on working his body so hard that his brain would no longer have the energy to dwell on Sadie's fascinating smile.

"Ouch," his twin said over the crackling static of a bad connection. "Is that a sign that things aren't going so great?"

"No," Heath said, bare-chested, hunched over and breathing hard alongside a pile of boulders. The blazing afternoon sun bore down on him. His memory of his hostess dressed in denim Daisy Dukes made him hotter still. "As far as you're concerned, everything's fine."

"So, then, what's your problem?"

"You know the owner?"

"Sadie Connelly?"

"Yeah. What's the scoop on her?" Heath wanted to know.

"I don't know. I mean, she's supposedly a great chef and all. Why?"

"No biggie," Heath replied. It was just that for the first time since Tess had crushed his spirit he felt like his old self—at least in terms of his manhood. If *manhood* was even a word? Something about Sadie Connelly intrigued him. Attracted him. Made him want to slough off the funk he'd been mired in and take another chance on life. All of which should have been a good thing. But seeing how the last time he'd felt any of that he'd been burned, Heath wasn't sure whether he should be happy about rejoining the land of the living or scared as hell.

"You still there?" A car revved in the background.

"Uh-huh."

"You don't have a thing for this woman, do you? I mean, you've only been there a few hours."

"No. No way, man. She's a looker and all, but you know me. I'm single and lovin' it."

Hale snorted.

"What?"

"Layin' it on a bit thick, aren't you? From the few pictures I've seen of her, you could do worse. Only, seeing how you're supposed to be me, kindly refrain from fraternizing. It's against my professional code of ethics."

"Who said anything about fraternizing?" Heath asked, scooping up a stone and skipping it across the lake's glassy surface.

"Okay, great," Hale said over more engine noise. "Look, I've got to go, but I did remember one thing about Miz Sadie and that's that I'm pretty sure she's engaged, which definitely puts her off-limits. Meaning, you might wanna check for a ring before trying out any more of your patented moves." Hale, who was the family playboy and knew full well that Heath didn't have any such thing as *moves,* patented or otherwise, finished by laughing.

"Screw you."

"Lighten up. I'm just joshing, man. I'm sure you've got all the right stuff to make Miz Sadie swoon. Only, don't do it. It'd be bad for business."

"I've gotta go," Heath said, eyeing the idyllic inn across the lake. Maybe two more times around the dirt trail would make his head a little clearer. Sadie engaged? No way. But then, if she was well on her way to tying the knot, that'd probably be best for all concerned. Especially him!

"Fine," Hale said. "Only, don't let me down, bro. I've got a lot riding on this review."

Then you should be here, doing it yourself.

"I'M IMPRESSED," SARAH called from the lakeside gazebo, where she stood with a cold bottle of water in her hand. "You're speedy."

Heath gave her a nod, stopping to brace his hands on his knees. "And if that water's for me, you're my new best friend."

"Mmm…" She wagged the bottle, then tossed it his way. "Looks as if you just got yourself a pal."

He twisted open the white plastic top, then half emptied the bottle in three swigs. "This hits the spot. Thanks."

"You're welcome. I was picking herbs when I spotted you across the lake. I figured you'd need a cool drink when you finished."

"You figured right." He eased onto the wide gazebo steps, rolling the sweating bottle across his forehead.

Sarah tried doing the polite thing, looking away from his chest, but up close and personal like this, well… She licked her lips. The man was magnificent. Broad shoulders, sharply defined abs and pecs. Shane might design computer games for a living, but he certainly wasn't your garden-variety computer geek.

Trying to play it cool, Sarah said, "I'm pretty much a slug."

"Oh?" Shane arched a brow.

Her cheeks reddened when she caught him appraising her form.

"Looks like you do all right in the gym to me." Had it not been for the playful light in his eyes and the fun in his tone, she'd have—what? Thought that he was flirting? So what if he was? Bringing him water hadn't been entirely altruistic. Yes, it might have been something her sister would've done, but Sadie would have already been on her way, eager to meet the next guests' needs before they'd even known they'd had them.

Sarah, on the other hand, found herself wanting a little more than to pick up their earlier conversation right where they'd left off. "Thank you," she said at last. "I think."

"You're welcome. So…" He took another swig of water. "To what do I owe the pleasure of your company? I'd've thought you'd be knee-deep in inn business all afternoon."

Sadie would have been. Not entirely trusting Sarah's innkeeping prowess, however, her twin had made certain extra help was on hand, so that the demands on Sarah would be kept to a minimum. "I, uh, have the pleasure of having a full staff tonight, leaving me to spend more time getting to know my guests."

"And have you?"

"What?"

"Gotten to know anyone especially well? Say, Mr. and Mrs. Standridge?" The twinkle in his eyes let her in on a secret. That apparently he, as well as she, would rather eat tacks for dinner than spend free time with the disagreeable couple.

"They seem sweet," she said, slipping into the perfect-innkeeper role, in which she enjoyed all her guests' company. "Just a little demanding."

"Uh-huh." He bottomed-up the water.

"What are your plans for the rest of the afternoon?"

He shrugged. "Nothing much, just lazing around. Unless…don't suppose you'd want to show me around the place? Give me an exclusive into the behind-the-scenes gossip? Who's dating whom?"

"I'll be glad to show you around, but if it's gossip you want, the place is pretty dull. Aside from a part-time gardener and the guy who tends bar Saturday nights, it's an all-women staff."

"Damn." He feigned disappointment.

And Sarah feigned not having delirious butterflies winging about inside her at the prospect of getting to know Shane Peters better.

"THIS…" HEATH'S TOUR guide said with a flourish, "is our world-famous Tennessee Williams Suite. He dropped in himself to give it his official seal of approval."

"I thought you'd only been in business five years?"

"True."

"But he died, like, in the early eighties."

"Your point?" She asked the question with a straight face, but crinkles at the corners of her pretty eyes told him she knew she was full of bologna.

"I stand corrected." He also stood in awe. He'd never noticed decor one way or the other before. Don't get him wrong—he appreciated a comfy sofa the same as the next guy, but whether that sofa was red, yellow or purple didn't make a difference. This room, however—make that the entire inn—proved to him that Sadie wasn't only a great cook and gardener but an interior designer, too. Was there anything the woman couldn't do? "You must've meant that Mr. Williams's ghost gave the room his endorsement."

"Yes. That's absolutely what I meant." She made no effort to hide her grin, for which—as cute as it was— he was appreciative.

The suite had been done in a New Orleans French Quarter theme, with plenty of deep red velvet and a black wrought-iron bed. The combo sounded risqué, but Sadie had made it work, right down to the gold satin tassels on the drapes.

"Do you put a lot of couples in here?"

"Why do you ask?" she teased. "Find it steamy— just like the city?"

"A wee bit." Reddening, he fanned the neck of the white St. Louis Cardinals T-shirt he'd donned for the tour. "What's our next stop?"

"Well," Sarah said, stepping out of the bedroom

and closing the door. "You've now seen the whole place. What do you think?"

"Pretty sweet. I'm still in awe that you did all of this yourself."

"My parents helped when they had time—and my sister, Sarah. She's awesome. Very handy with a hammer, nails and paintbrush."

"She older or younger?"

"Younger, but not by much. How 'bout you?" she asked, leading him down the back staircase. "Have any brothers or sisters?"

"One slightly older brother. And when we were little, he lorded it over me."

"I know the feeling." Glancing over her shoulder, she shared a laugh with him, and in that moment something about her smile, her bright eyes, gave him the keenest craving to kiss her. Yes, it was bad for business, as his brother had said, but seeing how the woman need never know of the switch or the review, would just one kiss hurt?

His conscience said yes.

The part of him that was eyeing her sweet derriere screamed for him to go for it.

"There you are," a sixty-something bottled redhead said from the bottom of the stairs. Not that he was a hair-color expert any more than he was an interior designer, but the orange-pink glow kind of gave it away. "Where've you been? If you plan on serving anything beyond peanut butter and jelly for dinner, girl, you'd best be movin' along." The woman's all-white chef's garb, combined with an ample figure, called to mind the Stay-Puft Marshmallow Man. But then, he didn't have a middle-European accent, did he? Did he even speak at all?

"Sorry," Sarah said. "I lost track of time."

"Easily done with a good-looking man by your side. Introduce me."

Heath tried to ignore their proximity in the cramped hall outside the kitchen.

"Helga," Sarah began, "meet Shane Peters. He's the current resident of the Mark Twain Suite."

"Nice to make your acquaintance," the older woman said, oddly rubbing the center of her forehead. "Are you alone here at the inn?"

"'Fraid so."

"Then it's a good thing our *Sadie* has been keeping you company."

"Yes, ma'am."

"Do you have a girlfriend?"

"Helga!" Sarah protested. "That's completely out of line."

"What?" the woman complained. "My all-seeing eye says the two of you may make a good couple. It never lies, you know."

"You can't just go around asking men questions like that," said Sarah. "And, Shane, just to let you into the loop, Helga comes from a long line of Gypsies."

"Not *just* Gypsies," Helga corrected. "True visionaries who hold the power to see deep into the future. Therefore it is my obligation to tell a man and a woman whether or not they would be suited for marriage."

"M-marriage?" Sarah sputtered. "Helga, stop this right now."

"It's all right," Heath said, fighting to hold back a

laugh. "As a matter of fact," he said to the older woman, "in answer to your prior question, yes, I am very much single. But what about Sadie here? Seems like I read somewhere that she's engaged."

Chapter Three

It took Sarah a good five seconds after Shane Peters had asked the question to remember to breathe. What should she say? Yes, Sadie was very much engaged, but if she said so, there went her opportunity to get better acquainted with a seriously cool guy. Then again, beyond casual conversation, she wasn't supposed to fraternize with the guests. If she admitted that her sister was engaged, then that gave her a noble "out" to keep things on a strictly professional level, instead of pulling him in for a forbidden kiss.

Something her guilty conscience had been contemplating for at least the past fifteen minutes!

"She *was* getting married," Helga said, "but that boy turned out to be no good. I say, Sarah—I mean, Sadie—forgive me, I'm all the time getting them confused. I say, that boy, he's no good for you. You must break up right away. My eye sees all."

Nodding, Heath said, "Sounds like sage advice."

"Oh, it was," Helga said with a firm nod. "Now you two go drink some lemonade—or whatever it is you do these days."

"Helga!" Sarah's cheeks flamed.

The cook, who was like a second mom to her sister, waved off Sarah's concern. "I thought you were loafing, which is why I asked for help. But if you have romance, then I say focus on that."

"Helga!"

"Thank you for your concern," Heath said to the woman, who was clearly deranged. His hand clamped Sarah's shoulder, giving her a gentle squeeze. Awareness sparked through her. "And also for the offer of lemonade. But I need to make a few calls and take a shower before dinner. After that—" he cast Helga a wink "—I just might take you up on the offer of romance."

"For Miss Sadie—not me."

"Aw…why would I want her now that I've met you?"

As Helga shot him a dirty but pleased look, then hustled back to the kitchen, Sarah said, "I'm so sorry about that. Usually she reserves all that *seeing-eye* mumbo jumbo for family. Who knew she fancied herself a matchmaker?"

"Question is," he asked, "do you want to be matched?" After a quick kiss to her cheek, he was off, whistling his way back up the stairs, as she stared rapturously at his departing backside.

One hand on her hip, the other cupping a tingling cheek, Sarah pondered the question. Helga barging in on them had been both good and bad. While it was annoying and highly unprofessional of her to have stuck her nose where it didn't belong, she had, in a sense, cleared the way for Sarah to pursue Shane—if that was what she wanted. So was it?

Greg hadn't just made a mess of her heart but of her head, too. How many times in recent months had she told herself she'd never, ever trust another guy? And yet here she was, unfathomably intrigued by this man whom she hardly knew yet felt as if she'd always known.

Could Helga's all-seeing eye be right? Was it fate that had led Shane Peters's date to turn down this weekend, so that the two of them could meet?

Sarah groaned and headed for the kitchen.

After Helga chewed her out for letting Shane go— even temporarily—she assigned boring cutting, chopping and dicing tasks that required no talent and left plenty of time for thinking.

Sarah had spent her entire career exploring other people's hopes and dreams, doing the necessary math to estimate how much money it would take to make those dreams reality. She'd heard about everything from retiring to a remote tropical island to refurbishing railway boxcars and turning them into mountain or backyard retreats.

She'd always been fascinated by people's dreams. The secret, giddy goals that drove a person out of bed each morning and into the rat race of modern life. Everyone had a different pot of gold at the end of the rainbow. But what was hers?

In the beginning, she had wanted the usual. Hubby, kids, white picket fence. But then she'd gotten burned and her world had crumbled.

Everything that she'd thought was real had turned out to be a lie.

Until now, when a gorgeous, funny, warm guy

named Shane had kissed her. And she wasn't even sure if that was a good or bad thing.

"C'EST MAGNIFIQUE," Mr. Standridge said, smiling with a flourish of his fingertips to his lips. If Sarah did say so herself—though she hadn't had a blessed thing to do with it—Helga's painstakingly prepared *flan au saumon et aux asperges* tasted divine. Thank God, on her latest trek around the dining room all guests present seemed to agree. "My wife and I have traveled the whole of France, and never have I experienced anything quite so exquisite."

"I couldn't agree more," Mrs. Standridge said, placing her hand on Sarah's arm. "Truthfully, honey, after the slow service at lunch, I was a bit concerned. I see now you must have been having an off moment. Everything all right?"

"Couldn't be better," Sarah said with an airy smile, brimming with confidence—easy enough to do with the kitchen in Helga's more-than-capable hands. Sarah was especially relieved to have spotted Shane with her peripheral vision, wolfing down his meal. At least Helga hadn't sent him packing. Lord, the man was gorgeous—in a strictly professional way.

"If it's no bother," the widow Young asked in a wavering whisper as she pushed aside her plate, "may I inquire as to what's for dessert?"

"Of course," Sarah said, giving the Standridges one last smile before moving to the other woman's table. Schmoozing was much simpler now that she'd relaxed, trusting Sadie's planning to make everything work. The slow service Mrs. Standridge had complained about had been the result of nerves, but plainly all Sarah's fears about running the inn had been a waste of energy. "For dessert, we'll be having *fraises à la maltaise,* which is a fancy name for strawberries marinated in orange juice and Cointreau."

"Wonderful." The widow actually clapped her hands with glee. Sweet as the woman was, Sarah refrained from rolling her eyes. These foodie types took their dessert seriously.

"Perfection," Mrs. Standridge tossed into the conversational salad.

Eyeing Shane, Sarah caught him grinning. Their gazes met and the result was exhilarating. That shared sense of consciousness. Even though they were a room apart, she felt as if he were right beside her—sharing her happiness in a job well done.

The meal wound on with the guests oohing and cooing over the gorgeous, meticulously carved orange bowls of marinated strawberries garnished with fresh mint. The honest part of Sarah wanted to drag Helga into the dining room to accept the praise she deserved, but instead the portion of Sarah that had sworn to imitate her sister graciously nodded and smiled, acting as if such wonders were all in a day's work. Which for Sadie, of course, it would have been.

Had Sarah tried something this fancy on her own, the guests would have ended up with results closer to runny Jell-O!

"Lively yet soothing," Mr. Helsing announced after his first bite.

His wife, after taking her first taste, closed her eyes and sighed. "Utterly dreamy. I agree that after lunch I thought for a minute about repacking our bags, but now I see how everyone who's raved about this place has been right. How do you do it?"

"I'm not sure I know what you mean," Sarah said, doing her best to imitate her sister's modest poise.

"I think what she means," Heath said, deftly sliding aside his empty plate, then dabbing that gorgeous, sexy grin of his with a white linen napkin, "is how did you manage to turn out a meal like this when you not only look cool and composed but have had so much time to fulfill our every need?"

"That's my job," she said, ignoring the way her stomach lurched at the lie. "Over the years, I've become a master of prep work. You know, chopping and dicing late every night, to ensure I can present my guests with unrivaled tastes and luxury they won't soon forget."

"I'd say you are now fully succeeding in achieving your goals. Well done," Mrs. Standridge pronounced.

"Here, here," said Mr. Helsing with a show of applause that his wife joined in on.

"Well," Mrs. Helsing said, "now that our appetites have been properly sated, would any of you care to join my husband and me for a round of canasta and a liqueur in the game room?"

Sarah crossed her fingers behind her back, hoping that everyone would agree—especially Shane. She'd only known him for one afternoon, and yet her awareness of him was all-consuming. She wanted nothing more than to spend the rest of the night—oh, heck, who was she fooling, the rest of the *weekend*—getting to know him better. Trouble was, she'd also fallen for Greg this fast, and look where that had ended up.

Could anyone say *disaster?*

After all the inn's guests had thanked her again for a lovely meal and then chattered their way into the game room where she'd promised to bring an assortment of after-dinner liqueurs, Heath held back.

Once they were alone, he cleared his throat. "You know, Sadie Connelly, I'm liking your smile as much as your fancy strawberry stuff. What was in it again?"

"Grand Marnier."

"That's funny," he said, scratching his head. "I thought it was OJ and Cointreau?"

Pulse racing at her stupid mistake, Sarah said, "Oops."

"Yoo-hoo! Mr. Peters!" Mrs. Young had found her voice. "I need you to be the other half of my pair."

"Duty calls," he said. "I presume your having forgotten your dessert's main ingredient was a simple mistake?"

"What else would it have been?" Her heart thundered.

"Relax," he said with a slow, sexy grin. "I'm totally joshing you. But just in case there's a hidden controversy afoot and there is more you need to confess, how about we meet up later so you can tell all?"

"KNOCK, KNOCK," HEATH said in the balmy darkness. While his head told him to steer clear of his beautiful hostess, the quickening of his breathing whenever she was near told him full speed ahead.

"Who's there?"

"I wanna," he said, strolling around the edge of the back porch, mounting the three stairs.

"I wanna, who?"

"I wanna congratulate you on having a bunch of happy guests."

From her seat on a padded wicker bench, Sarah laughed. "Congratulations to you for obviously having the great taste to have come to my fabulous inn."

She was surrounded by clay pots of sweet-smelling white, red and purple phlox. The only light was indirect and golden, escaping the kitchen, casting her in a soft glow. Heath hadn't thought it possible for her to look prettier than she had while she'd served their dinners, but he'd been wrong. At this moment, her smile shone radiant against the night.

He cleared his throat, then gestured to the wicker armchair across from her. "May I?"

"I don't know… This area is generally reserved for employees. You know how it is. I don't like my employees mingling with guests."

"Fair enough," he said, sitting anyway, crossing his legs so that his left ankle rested atop his right knee. He'd changed from the suit and tie he'd worn to dinner into faded jeans and a retro black Rolling Stones T-shirt. "But, you know, seeing how I helped with all those towels this morning, I think that qualifies me for back-porch privileges."

"I think you'd be right. But if you want a raise, forget it. Some of those towels had to be refolded."

"Ouch."

"Hey, I *am* the boss. If folks see me going easy on you, they may want the same special treatment."

"That means I already am getting special treatment?" He dodged when she tossed a floral throw pillow in his direction. "You are *so* getting reported for employee abuse."

The size of her grin said she didn't care.

Neither did he.

He should have been back in his room, making sense of the hasty notes he'd discreetly scribbled for Hale during dinner. But where was the fun in that? So far, his brother was right in that giving Sadie her five-spoon review was a no-brainer, leaving Heath with plenty of time to better acquaint himself with the brains and beauty behind the inn's perfection.

"Fan of Mick?" she asked, nodding toward his shirt.

Shrugging, he said, "More old-school than new."

"Me, too."

A few minutes' companionable silence was disturbed only by chirping crickets and an owl's lonely call.

There were lots of things Heath wanted to ask Sadie Connelly, but should he? After all, he'd already worked out the fact that he wasn't over Tess. What good would it do him to get to know Sadie better when he still had so much to figure out about himself?

"I know what you do for a living," she said, her voice quiet in the chilly night air, "but what do you dream about?"

Forehead wrinkled, Heath said, "I don't get the question."

"Come on, play with me. Everyone has dreams. Since you're in computers, do you want to be the next Bill Gates, for example?"

"No," Heath answered truthfully.

"Then what do you want?" Leaning forward, Sarah rested her elbows on her knees. The pose unwittingly thrust certain womanly parts of her anatomy up and out, making it hard for Heath to focus on those dusky martini-olive eyes of hers instead of the plunging vee neckline of her white blouse.

What did he want?

At the moment, he wanted a fantastic night with Sadie Connelly. Hot and wild. No strings. Because when strings broke, he was the one who got hurt.

Come on, his conscience ragged. *What happened with Tess was a one-time deal.*

Yeah, he fought back, *but that one time, I gave her my heart and soul. I wanted to have kids. Set up house-keeping. Buy a dependable car.*

Even worse, Sadie Connelly was off-limits. His brother might love racing on the side, but until Hale made enough cash with his car to quit his day job, Heath owed it to his twin to keep this gig strictly professional.

"I'm waiting," she said in that throaty tone of hers that was starting to be a major turn-on. "Dreams?"

This was sticky. Not only was Heath supposed to keep it casual between them but he hated lying. And so, on the fly, he carefully crafted a mingling of half-truths and deceptions, saying, "What I want is pretty simple. A few lucky career breaks have landed me more than enough in the bank, so…" He paused a moment to try and calm the nerve that was ticking in his jaw over the entirely true admission he'd decided to make. "Get out your violin, but deep down I guess I just want what lots of folks want. Security. To carry on the species."

"Kids? You want a wife and kids?"

"You don't have to sound so shocked," he said, frustrated with himself for being so honest. Hating to realize that her eyes, her voice wielded such power. Knowing that her disapproval would hurt him.

"No," she said with a rapid shake of her head. "You misread me. I meant it as a compliment. You're a good-looking guy, and I had you pegged for a party boy. You've probably got gorgeous women lined up to accompany you to glitzy parties all the time."

"Been there, done that," he said with a wry grin. "I'm getting old. Like a tortoise. Time to bale hay and mend fences and all that crap."

"For the record, you're hardly grizzled or old, and baling hay isn't crap," she said with conviction. "Thank you."

"For what?" Heath looked out to the brick patio, unable to deal with the impossible-to-read emotion that shadowed her expression.

"Being open with me." She fidgeted in her chair. Sighed. "Since you've been so straight with me, I guess I owe you the same courtesy. I used to want the same. Nice house. Two-point-five rug rats. I'd met the perfect guy—tall, dark and handsome, with this little dimple in his right cheek every time he smiled."

"Uh-oh," Heath said with a groan. "I'm taking it from your pinched expression that this story has one of those Oscar-type tragic endings—as opposed to the summer blockbuster happy type?"

"You like movies?"

"Love 'em. But back on topic. This guy break your heart? Want me to arrange a fish picnic for him at the bottom of the lake?" He nodded toward the breeze-dappled water that glistened in the moonlight at the garden's edge.

"How chivalrous of you," she said with a flirty bat of her eyelashes. "But he's long gone. Not quite as satisfactorily as the method you proposed. But I suppose the state pen has a certain charm all its own."

"Prison?" Heath whistled. "Damn, girl. What'd he do?"

"Oh." She absentmindedly twirled a lock of her hair. "Just a little embezzling on a pretty major scale. Throw in a dash of mail fraud, and he's vacationing behind bars for quite some time."

"Whoa. Remind me to stay on your good side." If only Heath could've been so lucky with Tess. Too bad for him, corporate espionage of her kind was oftentimes nearly impossible to prove.

"Sadly, I wasn't the one who shipped him downriver. I just lost my money—and heart—to the creep."

"Double ouch."

"Tell me about it. On the plus side, I can now sniff out a lying SOB at close range."

"Oh?" What were the odds of them both having been bitten by the same type of animal? The notion made for an odd sort of intimacy, knowing Sadie had been through a similar brand of angst.

Only trouble was that seeing how from the moment they'd first met Heath had done nothing but tell lies, not only was he in a sticky situation but it didn't say much about the effectiveness of her liar-detecting radar.

Heath wanted to blurt out a caution to her bewitching, trusting gaze, but how could he when at the moment he was the one from whom she needed to hide?

Still, it wasn't as if the favor he was granting his brother by posing as him was doing any real harm.

At the weekend's end, once he'd handed Sadie her five silver spoons, he'd come clean—about everything. Until then, knowing she shared his deep hatred of liars, he'd tread carefully and try to be as truthful as possible without ever mentioning his genuine reason for being at her inn.

Chapter Four

Sarah knew she should have shut up about Greg, but something about Shane Peters's kind eyes made her feel open and secure. Able to tell him anything. It was ridiculous in light of the time they'd known each other, but nonetheless it was the way she felt. Still, maybe she wouldn't feel quite so vulnerable if Shane shared a little of his own history, which he'd alluded to but hadn't really explained.

"Earlier," she said, taking a deep breath before launching her conversational plunge, "before Helga interrupted us, you mentioned that you'd been burned, too. I'm sorry about that."

"Thanks," he answered. "Like your Greg, my ex should've ended up in jail. Only, she didn't. Meaning that after she stole a seriously profitable game design from me and then sold it to my largest competitor, I didn't even get the satisfaction of hearing a judge say, 'Guilty.'"

"But I thought games as sophisticated as yours were a collaborative effort? Taking years to design? How could she do what she did without there being piles of evidence?"

"Thanks to my blind trust, it was all too easy." His sharp laugh was raw with emotion. "How'd she do it? The most insidious way possible.

"True, I have a great team that works with me, but only after an idea has been fully developed in my head. That stage alone takes me a good six months or more. The story line has to be plotted, villains created. Hell, whole worlds have to be created.

"You'd think over the years I'd have become more savvy about this part of the process, but nope. Instead of designing on the computer, where I'd have backups, I write everything longhand. You know, if I came up with a great idea in the middle of the night and didn't have a notebook handy, I'd just jot my thoughts on the nearest napkin or candy wrapper, then shove it in my bedside drawer until I felt like I had enough info to develop a formal presentation for my crew.

"Once I'd reached that particular stage on this project, Tess and I went out to celebrate. Danced till two in the morning. Came home to make love. Slept till ten—one of the benefits of being boss." Absent-mindedly rubbing his jaw, he stared off toward the lake. Though he didn't say another word, fury—and the same pain of betrayal that Sarah had felt over Greg—radiated from him.

"Reading between the lines, I'm assuming she stole your notes?"

"Yep."

"Your reservation has been on the books for a while, but you said your date's name was Susie. On the rebound?"

"Busted," he said with a feeble grin. "My date was,

um, really supposed to have been Tess, but it hurt me too much to even say her name. That's why I said her name was Susie. Lame, I know, but it was the first thing that popped into my head." His gaze darted away from her.

Poor guy. It angered Sarah to think of the misery that woman must've put him through. "It's okay," she said. "I totally understand."

"But anyway," Heath said with a sigh, "back to the story. The morning after our big celebration, over Starbucks and bagels, Tess told me she was really happy that I'd finished fleshing out my newest game but that I wasn't her type. Next thing I know, The Kill debuted under Jamestown's label." Shaking his head, he added, "They seriously botched it, too. Rush job with crap graphics and a million bugs. The worst part isn't that I could have made that game into one of the biggest sellers of all time, or even that she stole it from me. The worst part is how I'd trusted her." He tapped his index finger to his temple. "When your only product comes from your head, messing you up emotionally can really take its toll."

"I'm sure," she said, sympathy building for this man she hardly knew and yet felt as if she'd known for a lifetime.

"Since then, I've had a seriously tough time trusting anyone. You know, not feeling as if everyone's out to get me or has an ulterior motive behind the nice things they do or say. When you brought me that bottle of water this afternoon, my first inclination was to wonder what you wanted in return."

"But, I promise, I was only—"

"I know, you were being nice. Which is what nice

people do. But after getting mixed up with Tess, I forgot there's another whole part of the world out there that doesn't lie, cheat or steal.

"Another confession. During dinner tonight, I had a tough time believing you could look so good and yet produce a meal of that caliber." He chuckled. "When Mom does Thanksgiving, you'd think she'd been underwater for a couple hours, then dragged behind a horse through gravy-filled ruts."

While sharing a laugh with her guest Sarah couldn't help but think that that was how she truly looked after fixing even an ordinary weeknight dinner. Which was why she usually ordered takeout. On the inside, her tender heart hardened at the thought that lying to Shane Peters as she was made her essentially no better than his ex-girlfriend.

Oh, sure, she was only doing this to protect her sister. But now that the threat of being reviewed wasn't hanging over her head, she should come clean with the guy. Without Sadie's permission, however, she couldn't.

Seeing how Sadie would no doubt call before sunrise to make certain everything was okay, Sarah vowed to herself that as soon as she'd talked to her twin, she'd reveal her true identity, be honest.

Gladdened by the fact that this blossoming friendship would soon be free of lies, she teased, "Your mom would strike you from the Christmas list for dissing her like that."

"Hey, I didn't say her looks in any way affected the food, did I? Everything tastes great. It's just that by the time she's done, she doesn't look half as together as you did."

With a playful pose, Sarah teased, "You think I look good, huh?"

"Strictly in a professional sense." His rogue's wink had her pulse racing. Between those flashes of dimple that showed with each grin and the blueberry-colored eyes, Shane Peters was causing Sarah to forget her own troubles. In fact, she was well on her way to becoming a smitten kitten.

"Good," she said. "Good, that is, that you're professional. I appreciate that."

"Likewise," he said with an earnest expression. Leaning forward and taking her hands in his—and in the process setting off fireworks of awareness and hope—he said, "Seriously, thanks for listening. Since Tess and I broke up, I've had a tough time reeducating myself as to the fact that not every woman's intent on running my life. I hardly know you, yet something about your eyes, your smile, tells me you could *never* cause that much pain."

Grimacing, Sarah replied, "Seeing how I pretty much feel the same way about *my* ex, I'd propose a toast, but at the moment I'm fresh out of anything to use." She raised her empty wineglass in a salute, praying humor would conceal her galloping heart. Dear Lord, she couldn't wait to tell him the truth.

At the very least, he ought to know her real name.

"Want me to head back to the bar for a fresh bottle?"

Yes, squeaked the forgotten voice of the woman who actually enjoyed a man's company. But the part of her that was committed to portraying Sadie politely said instead, "Thank you so much, but I've got a big day planned for tomorrow and I should get to sleep."

"You have to get up early for all that kitchen work?"

"Yep. Chopping and dicing and kneading. Then, after breakfast, the housekeeping begins. You haven't met Kim Foster—she's the person I thought you were when you helped me with the towels. Anyway, she gets here at the crack of dawn and she sets a tough toilet-scrubbing pace to keep up with."

"Sounds exhausting."

He had no idea!

"What led you to this kind of work instead of some nice, dull office job?"

What led me here? Sarah suppressed a laugh, hating the fact that she was once again on the verge of lying through her teeth. "I, um, always liked playing house as a kid. Hosting elaborate tea parties for my dolls and my friends. When I was a little older, I was always re-arranging and decorating my room. What can I say? I love making people feel warm and relaxed when they're in my home."

Nodding, her companion said, "From the happy campers I played cards with, it looks like you're doing a great job."

"Thank you. Coming from you, that means a lot."

"You're welcome." He pushed himself to his feet. "By the way, I'll send my bill for suffering through two hours of cards with the Standridges and the Helsings. Now, that widow Young, she's a hottie." He grinned and then stepped off the back porch and into the night.

Sarah knew she should get to bed. Even with Helga

and a full substitute crew arriving early, she'd still have to be sharp to meet Sadie's rigid expectations.

But then again, maybe not.

Now that the inn was for sure not being reviewed, surely her sister could relax her standards enough to allow Sarah this shot at happiness? It'd been so long since she'd even thought it possible to fall for another man, and yet now she realized it wasn't just possible but entirely probable.

With that in mind, Sarah couldn't resist lingering a while longer in the floral-scented night air, settling her feet up on the bench beside her and hugging her knees.

She'd have liked nothing better than to have opened that bottle of wine and then stayed outside talking with Shane Peters until they both got the yawns. Too bad that for the time being, until she'd been given the all-clear by her twin, what she'd like to do and what she was allowed to do were two very different things.

SATURDAY MORNING Heath found himself searching for Sadie Connelly from the moment he left his bedroom. He couldn't exactly put his finger on why, but something about the woman lured him like the night crawlers he'd brought for an afternoon's fishing on the lake.

Granted, he'd hoped to catch a nice bass and not a woman. But then, wait a minute. Seeing how he was the one being drawn to her, maybe his logic was backward. Kind of like his senses, since in the capacity of his brother, he had no business looking at anything but the woman's pastries.

Why, after the hell he'd been through with Tess, had

he finally met a woman he was not only attracted to but who could even relate to his misery in having come out on the losing end of relationship roulette? Why did she have to be off-limits?

Heading down the mammoth front staircase, Heath realized that at no point during Hale's initial endless speech about what he could and could not do had he ever mentioned *not* hooking up with the inn's comely proprietress.

Duh. Wasn't it kind of obvious?

Seeing how, if the two of them did end up together and then Heath recommended a five-spoons rating, it could be construed as not playing fair. Even if the inn totally deserved it. But then, with Sadie, nothing was fair. Starting with the fact that he suspected that, as much as he'd like getting back into the dating pool with a quick fling, nothing about her would be quick.

She was a lady through and through, and as such she deserved consideration above and beyond the kind a "liberated" woman only out for a single wild night might expect.

By the time he reached the sunny dining room, all the other guests were present, including Mrs. Young, who waved a yellow linen napkin in his direction, gesturing for him to sit across from her.

"I've wondered what's been keeping you," she said as he pulled out the chair opposite hers. While he would have enjoyed nothing better than dining alone—preferably on the stone patio, away from the blond temptation who was just beyond the kitchen door—in his role as the reviewer, he figured that joining the widow was the professional thing to do. "I thought maybe after breakfast we might play another round of cards."

"It'd be my honor," he said. "But could I have a rain check until later this afternoon? After breakfast I was hoping to get in some fishing."

"Oh," the widow said with a sage nod. "Of course. I hadn't realized fishing was an option here."

"Where there's water, there's usually fish. At least that's my motto."

Hands to her chest, the older woman leaned back and giggled. "My Charlie used to say the same thing. Hope you catch a big one."

Mercifully, breakfast moved along, but unfortunately with a freckle-faced teen doing the serving instead of Sadie.

The conversation was pleasant enough, with lots of cute snapshots of the widow's kids and grandkids over a meal of fancy eggs with a rich cheese sauce, along with prettily cut pieces of melon and a seriously decent potato side dish. Thick bacon and flaky croissants were big hits, as well. All of which made Heath more confident than ever that he'd made the right decision in going fishing. The inn's five spoons were a given.

"Thank you," Heath's dining companion said, setting her napkin beside her plate, then pushing back her chair. "This has been delightful, but after all this food so early, and with you off on an excursion, I think I'll lie down."

"You're not sick, are you?" he asked, placing his own napkin on the table and eyeing her with concern. An ill guest wasn't a good thing, and he'd probably need to make a note of it in Hale's little black book.

"Not a bit. Just feeling fat and lazy." She smiled, patting his shoulder on her way out of the room. The Standridges and the Helsings had already left, leaving Heath on his own, at least until Sadie hustled out of the kitchen looking more like a frazzled chef than a genteel innkeeper.

"Oh," she said, hands against her flushed cheeks. Her loose ponytail was streaked with flour. And her jeans and white T-shirt, covered by an oversize utilitarian white apron weren't exactly designer fare, although on her they looked great.

He thought about how long it had been since he'd had a Saturday-night sleepover, waking up Sunday morning with someone to share breakfast in bed. Was Sadie the type who'd occasionally be happy with a Pop-Tart or a bagel? Or was she one of those unique individuals who rose every day actually wanting to produce a big breakfast spread?

"I thought you'd have been done eating a long time ago."

"I was," he said, rising from his seat. "Just been hanging with Mrs. Young. She seemed lonely."

"That's awfully sweet of you," she said, adjusting her ponytail.

"What can I say? I'm a sweet guy." He shot her what he hoped was a semiattractive grin. Of course, it had been so long since he'd thought about using any of his male charm, who knew if he could even pull it off? Not that he was supposed to be charming the woman, but she was so cute that it was tough focusing on anything other than the adorable flour smudge just to the left of her chin.

Grinning, she shook her head.

"You disagree?"

"It's not that I disagree," she said. "It's just that…"

"Uh-huh. I'm so charming I've got you flustered, huh?"

"Anyone ever tell you you're incorrigible?"

"My mama."

"Figures." Her teasing smile told him he must be on the right track. "Only a mother could appreciate the likes of you."

"What's that supposed to mean?"

"Only that you, Mr. Shane Peters, are a flirt." She sidestepped him to bus the Helsings' table.

"Is that a bad thing?"

Stacking the dirty dishes, she said, "Depends on who you're flirting with."

"How about you?"

"Mmm…gimme a sec to think about it." Arms full, she sashayed right past him and back through the swinging kitchen door, leaving him alone with his thoughts in a fog of what he now recognized as Essence of Sadie. An exotic yet homey blend of eggs and bacon and something sugary and sweet with a hint of floral sophistication. But not fancy floral. More like simple. Like a just-picked daffodil. Damn, but he was starting to like this woman.

Which, considering how he was supposed to be his brother, presented a problem. Not necessarily an insurmountable problem. Just something he'd have to finagle his way through.

His hostess popped back through the door empty-handed. "You still here?"

"Where else would I be?"

"How about dreaming up some new ways to charm me?" she sassed, already at work on the Standridges' table.

"Interesting," he said, tapping his lips with his index finger. "But seeing how the sun is shining, I figured on something a little more outdoorsy."

"How about this—you make a list of ways to charm me *while* you're outdoors." She cast him a supersized cornball grin.

"Sounds doable, but I'd still rather fish. Wanna come?"

"Fish?"

"Yeah."

"Um…" She nibbled her lower lip. "Sounds like big fun, but once I finish up here there's laundry to do and beds to make and lunch to get started on and—"

"While I'm sure all of that's necessary in order to have the place in tip-top condition, shouldn't keeping guests happy be your top priority?"

"Ordinarily I'd say yes, but if we're seen together too often, don't you think the other guests might get jealous?" She'd finished with the last stack of dishes, then turned her back to the kitchen door, using her luscious derriere to bump it open. "I don't know," she said with a shake of her head. "It could be bad for business."

He trailed after her. "On the other hand, it could be great for business—especially mine. Oh, hey," he said, finding himself face-to-face with Helga, who was wielding a lethal-looking wooden spoon.

"No guests in kitchen," she said with her thick middle-European accent. "Even you, Mr. Handsome."

"Yeah, but—"

"No exceptions."

"Come on," Sadie said after leaving her load alongside the sink, dishrag in hand. "I'll show you the way out." Back in the dining room, she muttered, "Sorry—again. What Helga lacks in a sense of propriety, she makes up for in being the best assistant ever."

"No problem." Bracing his hands on the back of the nearest chair, he said, "So? Have you thought about it? Going fishing?"

Sighing, hands on her hips, she said, "As much as I'd love to wile away the afternoon with a fishing pole in one hand and a bologna sandwich in the other, do you honestly think my guests would understand?"

"The question you must ask yourself is, what's more important? Those other guests or *me?*"

Her expression was unreadable. Until she grinned, then walked away.

Chapter Five

On the inn's back porch, with the cool breeze working wonders on her flushed cheeks, Sarah took a series of deep breaths. Soon, she promised herself, the weekend would be over.

Translation: her crazy craving to spend time with this man she hardly knew would also be over. And then her life would again be perfect.

Reality check. Was it actually so perfect?

Sure, work was great, but what else was there? Night after night she sat at home moping about what had happened with Greg. It was not just about what he'd done but about how much she'd hoped he'd been *the one*. That special one-in-a-million guy with whom she'd happily spend the rest of her life.

So what did any of that have to do with why she was so upset about Shane Peters asking her to go fishing?

In her heart she knew by his light, flirty tone that all he wanted was to spend the afternoon with her—not a lifetime. He wasn't Greg. And she was no longer the person she'd been when she knew Greg. She was no longer trusting and she could now sniff out liars from a hundred yards away.

That said—or at least thought—why was her pulse still racing?

Because, plain and simple, she wanted to go fishing. She wanted to chuck her responsibilities at the inn and spend the afternoon and the evening that followed getting to know Shane inside and out. Because he, for the first time since she'd been devastated romantically, had been the only man to make her feel even remotely interested in the opposite sex. Which presented a pesky problem.

The second the weekend was over, she could come clean with him. But what then? He despised liars. How was she supposed to broach the subject of them maybe going out for drinks or coffee or bowling? Then top off what would undoubtedly be a blissful evening with, *Oh, by the way, everything you thought you knew about me? All lies. Right down to my name.*

Yeah. That'd go over real well.

Especially since her morning call to Sadie hadn't exactly gone as planned.

"You want to what?" her twin had screeched. "Absolutely not! You are not going to tell him what we've done. He might not be the reviewer, but what if the reviewer just happens to pop in? They do that, you know. You can never be too careful."

Sarah, always having been the more logical of the two, didn't believe for one second that a reviewer was just going to appear. But in that one in a thousand chance that he or she did? Then what? How would she ever forgive herself if her blossoming romance somehow messed up Sadie's chance to have her inn positively reviewed in a national publication? Not only would Sarah be back at the beginning in her search for a great guy but Sadie would never speak to her again.

Worse yet, Sadie would be justified in holding a grudge for a good long time.

"Knock, knock." The kitchen's screen door creaked open and out stepped the last person she wanted to see. "Attila the Matchmaker said you'd be out here. I'm supposed to tell you her *eye* said fishing would be good for your constitution."

"Her *eye* knew this…how?"

"Don't ask me. I'm just the messenger."

Considering her companion's admirable deadpan expression, Sarah managed a strangled laugh. The man was a saint for not having already run far away screaming.

Turning from the rail to face him, she said, "Sorry for vanishing on you like that. Your invitation was sweet. I just…" Not sure what else to say, she flopped her hands at her side, wishing the entire weekend was over.

"Funny," he said, "how you're apologizing when that's what I came out here to do. At least that's what I'd been planning on before delivering Helga's message became my top priority."

"Of course," she said with a mix of solemnity and humor. "The *eye* cannot be ignored."

"Absolutely. But listen." He'd dropped the teasing tone and sounded earnest. "I understand you have a job to do. I didn't mean to pressure you into playing hooky. This is an amazing place, but it didn't get that way by you lounging about."

"You seriously have nothing to apologize for," she said. "But if you'll accept my apology, I'll accept yours."

"Deal." He extended his hand for her to shake. She

did but instantly wished she hadn't. His hand was much larger than hers. Rough. Rugged and manly—which didn't make sense, seeing how his job wasn't exactly the manual-labor type. He held her hand a second longer than was probably necessary. Not that she minded. Just that she'd noticed. In the same way she couldn't help but notice every part of him, from his amazing eyes to his unruly dark hair to the hint of shadow on his jaw—even though when she'd seen him first thing that morning she'd been pretty sure he was clean shaven.

When he finally released her hand, she averted her gaze, not wanting him to catch even a glimpse of how much his touch had affected her. Clearing her throat and going back to deadheading a pot of bright orange marigolds, she asked, "What else do you do besides play around on your computer?"

"What do you mean?"

"Your hands," she said, tossing a few bedraggled flowers over the porch rail and into the azalea bushes. "They're pretty rough for a guy who just sits around making up monsters."

"Oh…" He laughed. "Weekends, I rock climb. It sometimes gets dicey, but it takes the edge off."

"Sounds fun. I've always wanted to try it."

"It's a great workout, but you have to stay focused. It's not like jogging in a park. You can't just zone out."

"Sure." She glanced up at him, noticing how the red polo shirt he wore over his khakis clung to his pumped shoulders. Her mouth mysteriously dry, she licked her lips. She suppressed an urge to curve her fingers over those meaty shoulders of his, testing for herself to see if they felt as good as they looked.

"I'd love to take you sometime. That is, if you ever get a weekend off from here."

"I wish." She wrinkled her nose. "But maybe. Who knows. We'll have to see if we can work something out."

"Great. Arkansas has some awesome state parks to rappel in."

"That does sound fun." Mmm…what could be better than a whole day spent watching him all hot and sweaty and… She didn't mean to cast him such a huge grin, but something about him made her happy. She wasn't sure how she'd spin the fact that she wasn't who she'd claimed to be when they'd first met, but it looked as if she'd have plenty of time to work up a plausible story. Something close to the truth but not quite.

He thumbed toward the lake. "Guess I'd better let you get back to doing what you do best."

"Sure." *Though I'd much rather go fishing with you.*

"If I catch something, will you cook it for me?"

Yikes!

Did Sadie offer that kind of service? Knowing her sister, probably. But Sarah didn't know the first thing about preparing a real live fish, as opposed to one that was all nice and headless, skinless and boneless from the supermarket.

"Absolutely," she said with a smile, hoping and praying that if the situation reared its ugly head, Helga would be kind enough to share a few pointers. "But you have to clean it first. I'm pretty sure there's a fish-cleaning station down by the boathouse."

"*Pretty* sure?" He raised his eyebrows.

Oops. That stupid sexy grin of his had her flustered again. "Okay, I'm *very* sure. It's just been a while since I've had enough leisure time to wile away an afternoon boating."

"Uh-huh," he teased. "Likely story. All right, then, I'll head off to catch dinner, and you don't forget your promise to cook it."

"Sounds a little sexist, don'tcha think?"

"Not if you view it as a man trying to provide for his woman." His blazing smile told her he was joking, but the fluttering in her belly told a whole other story.

AFTER TRADING BREAKFAST attire for fishing wear— Hale had told him he couldn't wear sweats and a T-shirt to the dining room—Heath fished for a while, but the hot sun beating down on his lucky fishing cap made him feel like a human baked potato. Also, he suspected part of the reason he hadn't had so much as a bite was that for the majority of the morning a pair of menacing swans had trailed the boat. Every time he'd cast, they'd hissed, barked and snorted. Thankfully they were currently just offshore, looking ready to peck Mrs. Helsing.

Considering his temporary swan reprieve, he should've cast again, but he was too hot.

Scooting from the bench seat to recline in the boat's bottom, Heath felt somewhat better. At least the aluminum hull cooled his back, and the sound of water lapping against the sides was relaxing. Aside from a few ducks bickering on the lake and the gentle breeze shushing through pines, oaks and maples on the shoreline, all was quiet.

The foam container of night crawlers was starting

to stink, but the water's faint musky-fishy smell was quite pleasant.

All this went a long way toward keeping Heath's mind off other smells. Such as Sadie's one-of-a-kind all-woman perfume.

Work had been pretty hectic lately, and he should have been happy for a peaceful interlude. But all he really wanted to do was get back to the inn. More specifically, back to Sadie Connelly, to see what she was fixing for lunch.

But what then?

For all practical purposes, he was his brother. He wasn't supposed to flirt with the innkeeper or really even have anything to do with her beyond casual conversation. So where did that leave him in his quest to get to know her better?

Pretty much right where he'd started when he'd broached the subject of a date sometime in the future. But even then, knowing she disliked liars every bit as much as he did, how was he supposed to explain that the guy she thought she'd met was a fraud?

"Hey!"

He glanced toward the boathouse to find Sadie waving.

Hands cupped to her mouth, she asked, "Still want company?"

Heck, yeah.

"Sure!" he hollered back. "Give me a sec to reel in my line!"

Five minutes later, he and his pair of swans had made it to the dock. "As cute as you look, I'd say you're my best catch of the day."

"Best, or *only?*" she teased, gingerly stepping into the boat holding a white wicker picnic basket. Wearing those denim cutoffs he'd first seen her in, a formfitting green T-shirt that matched her eyes and white sneakers, she looked every bit the fisherwoman and not the elegant innkeeper.

"Ha-ha. I'll have you know I've had plenty of nibbles, but those killer swans of yours keep scaring the fish."

"These sweet little things?" she asked, trailing her hand in the glassy water. When the nearest one hissed, she laughed, yanking her hand back to her lap.

Rowing to the lake's center, Heath asked, "What made you pick swans instead of a nice basset hound?"

"Swans are infinitely more elegant." She leaned back on her elbows, tipping her face up to drink in the sun. Every luscious inch of her legs stretched out in front of him, and a sweet strip of bared belly peeked out from between her shorts and her shirt.

"Not to mention mean," he said, trying to keep his mind on the conversation, instead of wanting to ease his hand along that tempting stomach of hers to see if it was even half as soft as it looked.

Eyes closed, she stuck out her tongue.

"So," he teased, "to what do I owe the pleasure of your not-so-pleasant company?"

"Helga. She wouldn't lay off the whole eye thing— meaning she must still be in matchmaking mode—and she ordered me out here. She said no guest should have to fish alone. She wanted to pack the lunch, but I told her I'd do it."

"Nice. What'd you bring?"

"My favorites. But don't tell anyone I prefer this

stuff to the fancy fare I, uh, prepare." She sat up, gently rocking the boat. From out of the basket she pulled bologna sandwiches on white bread, Chips Ahoy! cookies, Fritos and icy-cold Coca-Colas.

"Dang, girl, this is a regular junk-food feast. Well done."

"Thanks." She held out a sandwich. "Want one?"

"Sure." After they'd both munched quietly for a few minutes, then opened their drinks and taken deep swigs, Heath wondered aloud, "I don't get it."

"What?"

"How you serve up five-star meals, run an inn worthy of American royalty and yet eat this common folks' fare with glee."

She popped a cookie into her mouth.

"Well? Explain this side of yourself to me. It's intriguing. Almost like you're two different women."

He caught her wrist as she grabbed a handful of Fritos, before she'd gotten them into her mouth. "Sadie? You okay? The way you're shoveling food in pretty soon there's going to be three sides of you."

"Ha-ha. What can I say? I'm hungry." He freed her hand, and she tossed the chips to the swans. "As for there being two of me, I don't know. Sometimes I feel like there are. You know, one side a reasonably competent businesswoman, the other…" She glanced away and sniffled. Had there been tears glistening in her eyes? "I'm sorry." She looked back, this time wearing a brilliant smile. "Thinking about how gullible I've been makes me crazy."

Softening his voice, he asked, "Wanna tell me more?"

"I shouldn't," she said. "We hardly know each other, and—"

"Hey." He took her hand, lightly brushing her palm with his thumb. "I don't know about you, but I've found that it's sometimes easier to share things with virtual strangers than with people you know and love. That way, there are no expectations. Fewer disappointments."

She nodded and swallowed hard. "I caught Greg in dozens of little lies, but I always ignored them. All the time, my girlfriends were telling me to wake up. But it wasn't until I caught him out clubbing with not one long-legged, stacked brunette but two that I realized the guy was a snake. Not long after that, one of our mutual friends and a fellow investor in a gated community Greg had been planning showed up here at the inn, asking a lot of questions I couldn't answer."

"Like what?" He angled on the seat to face her.

"Like how Greg was managing to sell land that was part of a national forest."

"Huh?" Heath scratched his head. Wow, and he'd thought Tess was bad. "That's insane."

"My reaction, too," Sarah said with a half laugh. "At first, I told our friend Tom that he was crazy. I loved Greg. We were supposed to have a Valentine's Day wedding. My fiancé was a professional. He'd been in the construction and real-estate business for years. What I hadn't known, is that the business he'd been in was pretty shady. He owned three acres adjoining a national forest, where he'd set up a swanky stone cottage as a sales office to establish just the right tone of rustic elegance. Then he'd marked out fifty lots—each of them sheer one-acre perfection—selling for a hundred grand a pop. Clients walked through, instead of driving, on winding dirt trails. It was a forest wonderland, complete with slanted sunbeams, birds and squirrels. Folks couldn't get enough. That was in the area where I, um, used to live—near Branson, but flatter and not nearly as pretty, and this kind of real estate was tough to come by. Greg made a fortune. By the time buyers' architects starting filing for building permits, it was too late. Greg was long gone. Starting a brand-new scheme in Denver."

"Damn…" Heath shook his head.

"A lot of people were hurt financially—including me." She squeezed his hand so hard that it hurt, but Heath gladly bore the pain. "I'd planned a life with this guy. I'd shown him off to everyone, from my friends and parents and sister to my pastor. I adored him, and yet all those times he'd professed to feel the same way toward me, he'd only been playing me. Setting me up for a massive fall."

Sniffling, she asked, "Why, after all this time, does it still hurt? Why am I still weepy over a stupid, lying fool who doesn't deserve another second of my emotional energy?"

"Seeing how I still have my own moments over Tess, I couldn't tell you." Heath drew her hand to his mouth, then pressed a kiss to her palm. If they hadn't been on a boat in the middle of a lake, he'd have pulled her onto his lap, hugging her until her smile returned. "I'm so sorry that bastard hurt you. We hardly know each other and yet…I don't know…maybe because we've both been burned, I feel this kinship with you that I can't explain."

"It's the same with me," she replied. "Crazy but somehow right."

Lord, he wanted to kiss her, but as right as things felt between them, that still didn't fix the hell there'd be to pay if his brother ever found out—not to mention what Sadie would do when she found out. What would she think of him, having poured out her heart and then finding out that he'd been lying, too?

"Thank you," she said.

"For what?"

"Being here. Listening." Her smile lit up his world. "Showing me that not every guy's a liar." And then that world came crashing down.

"Yeah, well…" He cleared his throat. "How about we put all this depressing stuff behind us and catch some dinner?"

"Sounds great, only one problem."

"What's that?"

"I don't know how to fish."

"Eeuw!" Sarah shrieked thirty minutes later, impaling a squirming night crawler with her hook. "If you were a true gentleman, you'd have done this for me."

"If you're going to be a true fisherwoman, you have to learn to bait your own hook."

"When did I say I want to be a fisherwoman? All I really wanted was to have a picnic, thereby giving me an excuse to chow down on plenty of junk food."

"Which we just did while you presented me with a hundred reasons why you don't want to fish."

"Yeah, but…" She squeezed her eyes shut while completing the unpleasant task of hooking a worm. "You have yet to give me a compelling reason as to why I would want to catch my own dinner."

"Watch and learn," he said, taking her rod, then casting the bait, sinker and bobber in a wide arc that bypassed the swans and landed in a shady cove a good hundred feet away.

She whistled. "Impressive."

"Thanks." Only she wasn't so much talking about his cast but about the play of his muscular shoulders and back while he'd been in the act of casting. Lord, he was beautiful. Way better than any stinky old fish.

"Now what?" she asked when he gave her back the pole.

"We wait."

He baited his own pole, casting the line in the opposite direction.

"Hmm…" she muttered after they'd scorched in hot spring sun for what felt like an eternity. "This *is* fun."

"Just wait till you get your first nibble. I promise, from then on you'll be hooked."

"Yeah, but I'm pretty sure my flesh is boiling."

Rolling his eyes, he removed a long-billed khaki fishing cap from his head, settling it on her hair. "There, now that cute mug of yours is in the shade."

"Thanks."

"You're welcome."

"You think I'm cute, huh?"

"If I didn't, I'd never have invited you aboard."

The grin he shot her way stole what little remained of her breath. Dang, the man was good.

An eternity later, which she'd spent staring at Shane's back, finding it fascinating the way sweat dampened the valley between his shoulder blades, she had a new appreciation for the sport. But as enjoyable as it was to study the boat's captain, she couldn't help but think their morning on the water would be extra enjoyable if they were both to strip down to their skivvies and jump in.

"Look," he said, pointing to the spot where her bobber should be. "You've got something."

She had something, all right. A great idea of a much better way to pass the time!

"Well? Jerk up on the tip to set the hook and then reel it in."

Sarah did as Heath had told her to, but whatever was on the other end of the line was so heavy that it nearly ripped the pole from her hands.

"Whoa. What'd you do? Catch Jaws?" He shifted, straddling the boat's center bench, then motioned for her to sit in front of him. "Come here."

She did, gingerly stepping from the back of the three-seat aluminum boat to the center. Once she'd straddled the seat, too, being careful to hold tight to the rod, he put his arms around her, letting her reel but providing support should she need it. "What do you think it is?"

"I dunno. Some of these lakes have huge catfish. Could even be a particularly feisty bass."

Her pole was nearly bent in half. Sweat beaded her upper lip from the exertion of reeling in her line in the hot sun. Or was it being wedged against Shane that had her all hot and bothered?

"Whoa. See that?" The water roiled alongside the boat.

"Yeah, I saw it, but that didn't look like a fish."

He groaned.

"What's wrong?" she asked.

A thunk sounded on the boat's hull.

"What was that?"

"You don't want to know."

"Probably not, but tell me anyway."

"Okay, don't get excited, but I'm pretty sure there's at least a twenty-pound snapping turtle on your line."

"A what?"

"Hold the pole." She did, while he fished in his pocket, then pulled out a knife.

Thunk. Ker-thunk.

"Wh-what're you going to do?"

"Cut the line."

"What about the hook?"

"It'll eventually rust out. Unless you want to yank it out of whatever part of him—or her—it's stuck in? In which case, he might take a finger in revenge."

Thunk.

"That's okay," she said, queasy to think that she'd actually contemplated a dunk in the snapping turtle's domain. "Go for it."

He did, and though she'd have never admitted it aloud, something about his capable expression, the way he'd so calmly handled the whole turtle thing, made him even more attractive.

She'd lived on her own for nearly a decade and she was more than capable of taking care of herself, but after all she'd been through recently, it seemed like a lovely, decadent thing to put even something as minor as reptile trouble into someone else's hands.

Before her mind's eye flashed a wondrous image of the kind of husband or father Shane Peters would make. How sweet would he be, coming to his son or daughter's rescue? Helping them bait hooks and reel in their catches. Along the way, teaching lessons on nature and life and the finer points of junk-food selection.

Sarah knew that she and Shane were light-years from sharing that sort of family contentment themselves, but stranger things had happened. Trouble was, as perfect as all of that domesticity sounded, Sadie had made it plain that Shane Peters was off-limits.

Hmph.

Every bit of Sarah's contentment sank to the bottom of the lake.

Chapter Six

"Thanks," Heath said back at the boathouse, wrestling the life jackets out from under the boat's front seat. "Even though the morning didn't exactly go as I'd planned, it was fun."

"I'm still not convinced fishing's the life for me." Sarah grabbed the oars, but he took them from her.

"Let me."

"I can handle them."

"I know," he said, "but I've already kept you longer than I should've, and if you don't get into that kitchen ASAP, there are going to be lots of starving guests. Fortunately," he added, grabbing the picnic basket, too, "thanks to your thoughtful, always-prepared nature, I won't be one of them. But still, I—"

"Hush," she said, casting him another of her unreadable expressions. "You are off-the-charts adorable."

"Adorable." He winced. "I've been called lots of things, but never that—at least not since I was three."

She tossed her arms around his waist for a warm yet swift hug that he couldn't return with his hands full, even though he wanted to. Bad. She felt so soft and warm against him. And she smelled like a sun-kissed dream. He knew she'd never lie to him—she didn't have the capacity to lie. It simply wasn't in her nature.

"Thanks again for a wonderful morning," she said, "even if we did almost get capsized by a killer turtle."

When she stepped back, he rolled his eyes, fighting every instinct in his body that screamed for him to kiss her forehead. Her nose. That full, gorgeous mouth.

He shook his head. He had to pull himself together. For Hale and for himself. He wasn't in any shape to fall for another woman.

Yeah, but Sadie isn't just any *woman. She's special. Better than Tess had ever even dreamed of being.*

"That turtle was a sweetheart," he said.

"He wanted to bite me. I know he did."

"How do you know it was a he?"

Grinning, she said, "He looked a little like my old boyfriend."

Grinning right back, shaking his head, Heath said, "Go on, get out of here and into your kitchen to cook me something fabulous."

"Aye, aye, Captain." She gave him a saucy salute.

She was halfway to the gazebo when he called out, "Where do the oars go? They were just lying in the boat when I took it out."

"I don't know." She turned to face him. "Just stash 'em anywhere in the boathouse."

I don't know? How could she not know where she stored her own oars?

While Sarah headed for the kitchen, Heath frowned.

"WHAT DO YOU MEAN I have to make lunch myself?" With barely an hour until lunch was to be served, this was the last thing Sarah had expected Helga to say. She was hot and sticky and stinky and needed a shower. The last thing Sarah had time for was cooking. In the hope that she'd have time to hang out with Shane after lunch, she'd planned to repair her hair.

"I'm sorry, Sarah, especially after you and Mr. Shane had a romantic time with the fish. But my *bubbka* broke her hip. I've got to go to her." Helga took off her apron, tossing it in the dirty-linen hamper beside the door.

"But… That's awful about poor *Bubbka*. I feel terrible that she's hurt. But what am I going to do? You know I can't cook. I mean, I guess I could resort to serving all that stuff Sadie froze, but the guests won't like it near as much as what you prepare." Helga had to be pushing late sixties, meaning that her grand-mother must be coasting near a hundred. How could this woman who was devoted to Sadie just up and abandon her boss's twin at her greatest time of need? Sadie was like family, too, wasn't she? "All I'm asking for is an hour of your time. You said yourself your grandma's already at the hospital. She's not in pain and she's receiving excellent care."

Fluffing her brilliant pink curls, Helga grunted. "Your sister would never be so insensitive. I see why you are still single. No man have you. My eye now sees truth. You and this man?" Helga made a choking noise.

"Excuse me?" Hands on her hips, Sarah demand-ed, "What's that supposed to mean?"

As she slung a sturdy brown leatherette purse over

her shoulder, Helga said, "Your sister have nice man take care of her. You, she tell me, be a disaster at love."

"I am not. And anyway, what happened wasn't my fault."

"No never mind. If my *bubbka* is all right, I see you in morning." Chin high, keys jangling, Helga marched out the back door.

Pressing her lips together and counting to ten, Sarah reminded herself that she loved her sister. Sort of. Sometimes. At the moment, however, she was ready to call pizza delivery and wash her hands of this whole mess. At least Coco was still here. The bookish teen helped clean rooms, do laundry and, as per Sadie's written instructions, was currently popping fresh-cut tulips in the dining room's vases.

"Coco!" Sarah called, pushing open the dining room door. Ah, the girl was doing exactly what she should be doing and was even dressed neatly in starched khaki pants and a white blouse, with her long, dark hair pulled back in a neat ponytail. "Thank goodness you're still here."

"Where else would I be? I work until after the dinner shift on Saturday."

"Of course you do," Sarah said, thrilled to be in the reassuring presence of a junior Sadie. "Okay, listen, Helga had to leave, which puts us in serious trouble, so here's what we're going to—"

"Everything all right in here?" As if summoned by Murphy's Law, the last person on the planet Sarah would've wanted to overhear her strategy session appeared in all his dark-haired, blue-eyed glory. "Sadie, you sounded out of breath."

He was a sweetheart for caring, but just this once couldn't Shane Peters have kept his worries to himself?

Heart racing and utter panic crashing down on her at the prospect of not only being the inn's sole adult employee for most of the day but getting her cover blown to crumbs as fine as the ones in her sister's delicious graham-cracker crust, Sarah had a tough time finding her words. "Um, Shane. Hi. I thought you were down at the lake."

"I was, but it got hot. And then flies found my night crawlers and I really needed a beer. Got any?"

"Uh, sure," she said, taking a moment to search his handsome face for signs he'd overheard any of her brief conversation with Coco. "Dark? Light?"

"Dark, if you have it."

"Follow me," she said, praying she could get him settled fast and then figure out what to do about lunch.

On the way to the massive game room that Sadie had decorated to resemble an old-fashioned English pub complete with brass-railed bar and burgundy leather stools, Heath asked, "What was going on between you and your assistant? Not that I was eavesdropping, but I believe 'serious trouble' was mentioned? And why did Helga just peel out of the driveway?"

Racking her brain for her next half-truth, Sarah told him about Helga's *bubbka,* adding, "Not only am I short a kitchen helper but, um, I'm having serious trouble trying to decide whether to have flan or cheesecake for dessert."

From beyond tall windows framed by burgundy velvet drapes, there came the unmistakable sound of the Standridges clomping onto the inn's front porch.

The doorbell gave a happy jingle.

"What a wonderful walk," Mrs. Standridge said. "Quite invigorating."

"Yes," Mr. Standridge agreed. "It certainly stirred my appetite. I wonder what delicacies our innkeeper has planned for lunch?"

"Crap," Sarah said, accidentally giving voice to her feelings of panic. To Heath, she said, "Beer's in the fridge. Help yourself. Let me handle this dessert crisis and I'll be right back."

"Okay."

Dashing out of the game room and down the hall to the dining room and kitchen, Sarah threw open the kitchen door to find Coco by the sink, rinsing out the flower bucket.

Out of breath from her brief canter, Sarah blurted out, "Help…thaw…one of…those meals that Sadie froze. We'll have to work quick. Now, what time does Carly get here?"

Carly was Sadie's Saturday helper and the other waitress. Saturday night, the inn was open for business to anyone who happened to stop by—not just the overnight guests. Sarah's heart lurched, remembering her sister's fear that a reviewer might just drop in for a surprise inspection.

"Usually," Coco said, "Carly gets in around one, but last week she said she might be late this weekend. Her sister's having twins, and the shower was this morning."

"Ugh." Time ticking on the countdown to lunch, twins were the last thing Sarah wanted to discuss. Especially if the topic was her own twin, whom she currently despised! "Okay, Sadie gave me a list of what goes with what, but with Helga here I didn't figure I'd need it. Consequently, it's lost. Do you know enough about meal planning to cobble together a lunch?"

Coco tightened her face into a frown. "I suppose, but—"

"Fantastic. That's just what I needed to hear."

"But—"

"No time," Sarah said, hustling to the freezer.

"All I was going to say is that every once in a while Sadie calls in a guest chef. Maybe you could do that?"

"Seriously?" Sarah asked with her head still buried in the arctic deep freeze.

"What's it going to be?" Heath asked, popping his head through the kitchen door.

"What's what going to be?" Sarah asked, popping out. How was it fair that he looked gorgeous after his morning in the sun, when she felt frazzled and sweaty?

"Flan or cheesecake?"

"Strawberry shortcake," Coco blurted.

Sarah made a mental note to see that the girl got a raise.

"Sounds great," he said after a long swig of beer. "Glad you got it figured out, otherwise I'd've felt a gentlemanly obligation to help."

"I don't think so," Sarah said, clear of the freezer now and giving those solid shoulders of his a nudge. "You're an honored guest, and as such you will *not* be slaving away in here." Though it warmed her to think that he'd offered.

"I was only thinking of performing a few taste tests for you. You know, so I'd be qualified to give you an opinion of what dessert works best."

He dazzled her with a smile of such genuine intensity that her pounding heart altogether stalled. Attraction to the man flowed through her like sun-warmed honey, deliciously numbing her panic to the point where she almost forgot that she still had to find a guest chef for lunch.

"Listen," she said with her hand on his steely forearm, "I hate abandoning you again, but duty really does call."

Seeing how his free hand held his beer, he used the soft inside of his wrist to brush the top of her hand, making her wonder why she'd ever touched him. Was she now completely insane, on top of bedraggled? The chemistry between them was a living, palpable thing that she wanted so much to explore. Why couldn't she have met him under any other circumstances?

"Relax," he said, calming her icy panic. "You're amazing. I've never seen anyone juggle as many tasks as you, yet you always seem to top your previous efforts. Even without Helga's help, lunch will be awesome."

Nearly choking, Sarah said, "I appreciate your vote of confidence, but if I don't get in the kitchen ASAP, the only lunch I'll be serving is a platter of peanut-butter-and-jelly sandwiches."

He laughed. "No doubt with homemade potato chips, heart-shaped pickle wedges and an edible flower garnish."

Reluctantly, she released his tanned forearm, wishing and hoping that someday, somehow, they'd get their chance to meet again. The next time, with her being start-to-finish genuine. Beginning with her real name.

"NOW, MIND YOU," Branson Polk—the beefy, middle-aged redheaded chef from Catfish Heaven, said. "I don't do fancy. Sadie's the one 'round these parts who gets into all that flowery stuff. But if you want good pan-fried catfish, slaw and hush puppies, I'm your man. Otherwise closest you're gonna get to your twin is flying in some high-and-mighty muckety-muck from St. Louis or Kansas City."

Leaning against the stainless-steel counter with twenty-five minutes until her guests strolled in from their various pastimes for lunch, Sarah said, "You cook it and I'll decorate it. At triple your normal wage. Do we have a deal?"

They shook on one Southern-style catfish lunch with all the nonfancy trimmings.

While the chef organized the three assistants he'd brought along for the lunch battle, Sarah cut butcher paper to fit the kitchen door's tiny window and then took a deep breath. Crisis averted.

Now, with a little plate-decoration creativity and plenty of help from Coco, Sarah thought she just might ensure the survival of the Blueberry Inn's reputation after all.

FOR LUNCH, HEATH AGAIN found himself seated across from Mrs. Young, whose pale blue eyes looked so light that he wondered if she'd spent too much time in the morning sun, somehow making them paler still.

"Isn't this lovely?" she said, viewing her plate. What Sarah had managed to throw together on such short notice was nothing short of a miracle. Catfish nuggets rested in a boat made of a quartered pineapple. Alongside that were steaming hush puppies and coleslaw garnished with white, yellow and purple flowers that he'd seen in the garden just that morning. To complement the classic Southern meal, lively jazz flowed out of concealed speakers, spicing up the mood.

"It's pretty," he said. "But is it edible?"

"For shame, Mr. Peters. I'd thought you were more sophisticated."

Damn. Apparently not only were the dainty little things edible but everyone in the room seemed to know it except him. Winking, he said, "Of course I knew. I was just testing you."

She howled with laughter—well, as much of a howl as her reedy voice could produce. "Mr. Peters, really, I never suspected you for the type to have a wicked sense of humor."

Whew. Neither had he.

"Curious, though."

"What's that?"

"Why the kitchen door's window is covered. Do you think our Sadie's back there, whipping up some fabulous surprise?"

"Maybe," he said, not sure what to make of that bit of information. There'd been times when he was a kid that company had dropped in, catching their house at less than its best, and his mom had just shut bedroom doors—wishing that the kitchen had had one. Maybe Sadie hadn't had time to tidy the kitchen as much as she'd have liked and this was her solution. "I'm sure there's a logical explanation," he said. "Nothing overly mysterious."

Although now that he'd had a second to think about

it, was it a good thing for a public establishment to have a kitchen so messy that it needed hiding?

Out of deference to Sadie, for the moment he'd let the question lie, but he'd take a look later—just in case.

"You know," his dining companion said, "last time I was at an inn that served flowers I had dandelions, but these look to be a lovely allium mix. Wouldn't you agree?"

"Absolutely," he said, braving a bite. He was surprisingly pleased to find the little devils had a mild onion-and-garlic tang that was great with the slaw. Shaking his head and grinning, he found himself in awe of Sadie Connelly on so many levels that it scared him.

Somehow, some way, when this weekend was over, he had to get to know her as himself. Easily said, except that he'd made a big, hairy deal out of telling her how much he despised liars. Which was true, but seeing how he'd become one, it made for a bit of a problem.

The fact that he was lying for what was essentially a good reason, wouldn't make it any more palatable to the woman on the receiving end. Even though she didn't know it, Sadie Connelly had a tremendous amount riding on his—or rather his brother's—review.

When you thought about it, Hale was pretty much a jerk for even suggesting this switch. Granted, he'd said he wouldn't have done it if the Blueberry Inn's reputation hadn't already been so stellar as to be a guaranteed perfect rating. But still. Having gotten to know its innkeeper a bit, Heath felt dirty for duping her this way.

"Mmm…" Mrs. Young said, jolting him from his

thoughts. "This tartar sauce is heaven. Have you tasted it yet, Mr. Peters?"

"Not yet," he replied. "I'm still too busy with the slaw. Really *extraordinary*." He cringed at his word choice. Fruity, perhaps, but what the hell did he know about food? All he ever ate was frozen pizza and Subway takeout.

Truthfully, he couldn't give a flip about the food.

All he was really interested in was the chef.

"THANKS AGAIN," SARAH said, writing a personal check for the outrageous amount that her lunchtime chef had specified. "Now, are you sure you don't fix anything but catfish, because I seriously need help for dinner."

"Sorry," Branson Polk said, accepting the check, folding it in half and shoving it into the deep pocket of his white jeans. "But, really, catfish is my only claim to fame. Let me think about it, though, and possibly between me and my compatriots we can find you someone."

"Thanks," she said, hoping that her tone of desperation was making an impression on him. "Sadie left plenty of frozen meals, but I tried that yesterday and I'm pretty sure I might've accidentally served a few that were still rock-solid in the middle."

He gave her a sympathetic cluck. "Been there, done that. Whenever possible, fresh is best."

"Amen."

"You'll muddle through." He saluted her on his way out the back door. "Sadie wouldn't have entrusted you with this serious a task if she didn't have complete faith in your ability."

Oh? And what ability was that? Her newfound knack for dreaming up little white lies on the fly?

With Branson Polk and his team gone, the kitchen was back to being overwhelming.

Her mortal enemy.

Any fool could fudge her way through making beds, scrubbing toilets and washing a few towels. For sure, the weakest link in her innkeeping chain was the inability to cook. Having Helga called away was a crisis she hadn't foreseen. Whereas just hours earlier Sarah had felt confident she'd finish the weekend in a blaze of glory, she now felt seriously in over her head and afraid for what the next twenty-four hours might hold.

Chapter Seven

After casually inquiring as to his fellow diners' verdicts on lunch, Heath was pleased to find that with a resounding majority everyone had been suitably impressed. He'd assume by their not having mentioned it, no one, aside from his tablemate, had noticed the covered window—which was now *un*covered.

He'd glanced through the glass to see humming—spotless—efficiency.

To borrow Mrs. Young's word, *curious*.

But nothing to make an issue of.

Funny how the more he got to know Sadie Connelly, the more he wanted her to succeed. The more he was willing to overlook any of the tiny details he couldn't quite figure out. He barely knew the woman, yet he felt as if he'd always known her. As if their individual experiences with their exes had somehow fast-forwarded the normal getting-to-know-you phase.

After dutifully logging his notes on lunch in his brother's journal, Heath wandered out to the front porch, squelching the urge to invade Sadie's kitchen just to hang with her. Washing dishes, scrubbing counters—whatever. Seeing how his brother probably wouldn't do that, however, he figured it'd probably be best if he didn't either. Leaving him with nothing to do but twiddle his thumbs. Waiting for his next chance to see her.

The woman who undoubtedly, after learning of his deception, would never speak to him again.

The screen door creaked open and he looked up, hoping to see his hostess.

Bummer. It was just Mr. and Mrs. Standridge, bickering over whether to go rowing or antiquing.

"Mr. Peters," Mrs. Standridge said, "you seem to be a logical sort. Wouldn't you say antique shopping would be a better use of our afternoon than rowing?"

"Before dragging him into this," her husband said, "I can shop any day of the week. I thought we came out here for fresh air and relaxation."

Hands on her hips, she said snippily, "Shopping *is* relaxing to me."

"Well, not to me."

"See?" she said, directing her comment to Heath. "How can I possibly relax when I have to deal with his petulant demands?"

"Look," Heath said, making a time-out signal, "I'm thinking compromise is needed here. Trust me, the sun on the lake is brutal, so how about doing a little shopping while it's hot and then rowing later this afternoon, once it cools off?"

"Sounds reasonable," Mrs. Standridge said. "Arthur? That sound all right to you?"

Her husband grunted. "Get the car keys. If you want to shop, you'll have to drive."

Once the Standridges were off, Heath was back to moping on a wicker love seat, and then the screen door creaked open again—this time with better results.

"Hey," he said.

"Hey, yourself." With a sigh, Sarah collapsed onto the seat beside him. "I owe you a huge thanks for getting them out of my hair. Before they came out here, they were bickering in the dining room while we were trying to clean up and get things shipshape for dinner. Mrs. Standridge told me on her trip back in to grab her purse that you're the diplomat who settled the squabble."

"I'd hardly call myself a diplomat. More like a disinterested third party."

She laughed. "Regardless, thanks."

"So," he said, sliding closer, "I'm glad to see you pulled off lunch with your usual flair."

"Thank you," she said with a slight bow. "It was tasty. I had some myself after serving all of you."

"You don't usually eat your own cooking?"

She paled. "Sure, but, you know, sometimes after slaving in a hot kitchen you don't much feel like eating."

"Guess I can remember Mom saying the same."

"Where does she live?"

"Mom?"

"Duh." Sarah made a face.

"Damn, woman. You're a tough audience."

Grinning, she gave his shoulder a nudge. "That's what all my critics say."

"Right. Anyway, Mom and Dad still live in the four-bedroom ranch we grew up in."

"Your brother? Where's he live?"

"Um, St. Louis," he said, cursing Hale with every

breath. "Same as me. How about your sister and your folks—where do they live?"

"Um, my sister's in St. Louis, too. Mom and Dad sold the family homestead. Traded it in for a Branson condo. They both love fishing and country music, so they figured that'd be a great spot for both."

"True."

"Well," she said with her palms flattened on the seat cushion as if she were about to push herself up and leave. "Guess I should get back to work. The reception area needs dusting, the plants need watering and it's never to early to start thinking about dinner."

"So soon? Aren't you allowed even a short break?"

She laughed. "With Helga gone, there will be no rest for the weary."

"I thought the saying went, no rest for the wicked?"

"You implying I'm wicked?" she asked with a wickedly pretty grin that made him want to get to know her all the more.

"Shoot," he said, ducking his head, "I don't know what I'm saying. Just that I wish you'd take the next hour or so off and make like the Standridges and go antiquing with me."

"Okay, assuming I could spare the time—which I can't—why on earth would you go antiquing?"

She'd relaxed again. Good, because he wanted her out here with him as long as possible.

"Stupid, really. Embarrassing, even, since it's not very manly."

"Come on," she teased, "seeing how you rock climb, too, I would think that gives you plenty of extra testosterone to counteract your feminine side…the one that *adores* antique shopping."

"That tongue of yours is so sharp you could use it to slice a tomato."

"Oh, now that's a compliment if I ever heard one," she tossed right back. "So? What are you looking for in antique emporiums in my part of the country?"

He could've lied, but instead he went for the truth, knowing he was safe in assuming she'd never know such an intimate fact about Hale. "When my brother and I were kids, Mom and Dad would often take us to the St. Louis Zoo."

"Us, too," Sarah said. "It's still one of my favorite things to do when it's not too hot or cold."

"I haven't been in years," he said. "Maybe we should go together."

"Sounds like a plan. But for now, get back to your story."

"Okay, well, every time we went, our folks bought me those little wax animals. You know, the ones made in a machine while you watch?"

"Sure. I had about ten of them when I was little."

"Yeah, well, me, too. Only, one day when I was— I don't know—eight, maybe nine, I was playing with mine out by a creek, when a gang of my friends came over and asked if I wanted to go ride bikes with them. I said sure and left my animals, figuring I'd come back for them later. Only, when I did, they were all gone, washed away by a storm."

"Oh, no." Sarah comforted him with a hand on his knee. "I'm sorry. I hate to think of you as a sad little boy."

With a bittersweet chuckle, Heath said, "Mom did,

too, which is why she got me started collecting antique cast-iron zoo animals. They're hard to find, but I'm up to about twenty different breeds now."

"What's the latest acquisition?"

"Polar bear."

"Sweet."

"Yes, he is." As was sitting here on the shady front porch, shooting the breeze. Heath spent so much time in his office brooding over what might have been with Tess, then despising her, he'd nearly forgotten the simple pleasure of enjoying a woman's company. "So? You accompanying me on my latest safari?"

"I want to, but…" A myriad of unreadable emotions flashed across her face. Clearly she wanted to spend the afternoon with him, but pressures from the inn tied her down. "There are so many chores to tackle around here. Plus, getting ready for Saturday-night dinner's a pretty lengthy process and I like to make it extra special. Especially as I have reservations for five other couples who are coming out from town."

"Staying the night, too?"

"No, thank goodness—just for dinner. But you can see where that adds to my load."

"Sure," he said, covering her hand—which, amazingly, was still on his knee. She'd surprised him by expressing relief over guests not staying the night. You'd think the added business would improve her bottom line. Was this an indication of how overwhelmed she was by the inn's hectic pace? That she was stressed to the point of turning away guests? "I understand. Rain check?"

"Absolutely."

"Do you ever get tired of this?"

"What do you mean?"

He looked toward the flawless rolling expanse of lawn and the pristine gardens beyond. "All of this. It seems like a huge responsibility. Not just the upkeep of the inn itself but having to fix three squares a day for strangers."

Her expression was sad for a fleeting moment, and then she shrugged. "You get used to it. Of course it's a lot of work, but mostly it's fun. I get a lot of pleasure from seeing my guests happy."

"I'm sure. But inside—" he tapped his chest "—don't you ever feel trapped?"

"Truthfully, at the moment, when I'd much rather spend a leisurely afternoon getting better acquainted with you, yes. But usually no. I'm quite content puttering along with the daily care of this big old place."

"Fair enough." He stood. "Guess, then, I'd better not take up any more of your time. I'll leave you to it."

"Guess so."

Was that the hint of a sigh he'd detected as she'd bowed her head? Good. He wanted her to feel as disappointed about their afternoon apart as he did.

As HEATH WANDERED through a converted grocery store that claimed to be "Winchester's finest antique mall," he thought again about the fact that over the course of the morning and afternoon a few things about Sadie hadn't added up. Their picnic junk food—where had it even come from? Not knowing where the inn's oars were kept. The panic at having to function without Helga. The two women didn't even seem all that close, yet apparently Sadie relied heavily on the older woman. The covered kitchen window. Even more disconcerting was their recent conversation. Her admission that sometimes she felt trapped.

It seemed inconceivable that a woman with her phenomenal skills wouldn't enjoy her work. Every inch of the inn appeared to be the result of a love of all things domestic.

The antique store reminded him of the inn, in some ways. The way it'd been set up in homey vignettes, showcasing a bedroom here and a living room there, right down to vintage mannequins sporting appropriate clothes. Were Sadie to design a store, she'd have done it with this degree of style, he thought.

A mannequin wearing a voluminous green taffeta ball gown caught his attention. The dress was the same shade as Sadie's eyes—as was a matching green crystal necklace and earring set displayed nearby. Not thinking, just reacting to the memory of Sadie's olive-green eyes, Heath called over the clerk to help with his purchase.

After paying, he headed outside, stashing the jewelry in his Jeep's glove box, where it would wait until the right moment. Which, for all Heath knew, might never happen.

The gift was impulsive.

Pricey.

He wasn't even sure if it was appropriate, given how short a time they'd been acquainted. Funny thing was, he didn't care—on either count.

Pretty obviously, the reason Sadie wasn't acting like her normal self was connected to her split from her ex-boyfriend. Not that Heath had known her long enough to be able to gauge her so-called normal self, but any idiot could see there were times she didn't feel at ease in her own surroundings.

Heath had planned on heading back to the inn, but now he thought better of it and aimed for another antique store a half block away.

Across the street, which was lined with stately oaks and historic brick storefronts, the Standridges stood and bickered—loud enough for him to hear. Not specifics, just general grumpiness.

When Heath grew older and was married, he didn't want to be like that—arguing all the time. Instead he wanted to stroll tree-lined streets, holding hands, reminiscing. Smiling.

And it wasn't some random woman's smile that came to mind but Sadie's cute grin.

Part of her problem no doubt stemmed from feeling pressed for time. And why had she been short of time?

Him.

He shouldn't have been so insistent about her going fishing with him that morning. He *shouldn't* have been insistent, but seeing what a great time they'd had, he was glad he'd enticed her onto the boat. From here on out, however, he vowed to let her do her thing with the inn.

Then, once the weekend was over, he'd explain the switch, and if all went well, they wouldn't argue but would laugh the whole thing off.

Right. And then they could retire to the inn's front porch to watch pigs fly.

"You haven't done any more flirting with that single guest, have you?" Sadie's condemning tone made it clear what she expected Sarah's answer to be.

"Um, no." To be able to give her sister the response

she wanted, Sarah crossed her fingers. Flirting? Never. Why would she want to flirt when there were fun things like vacuuming and toilet scrubbing to do?

"Whew." A relieved sigh could be heard across the static-filled cell line. "Okay, so explain the problem?"

"Helga's *bubbka*'s in the hospital with a broken hip."

Sadie gasped. "Is she going to be all right? I adore *bubbka*."

"She'll be fine, but the main reason I called is that I'm worried about tonight's dinner. We've had a bunch of reservations come in from locals and…" Sarah debated about even telling Sadie the next part.

"And?"

"Well, one of the reservations was for a single woman. You don't think she could be that reviewer you've been looking for, do you?"

Groaning, Sadie said, "Anything's possible. Have you called Josie yet?" Josie was one of Sadie's closest friends, a gourmet chef, and she ran a small, chic vegetarian bistro in nearby Drover's Ferry.

"Duh. She's got measles."

"No way?"

"Yes way. I've got plenty of frozen food left, but with the potential reviewer coming, I figured you might want tonight extra special."

"You've got that right. Okay, let me think…" For a long time Sarah heard nothing but the faint sound of a boisterous crowd and the "Chicken Dance" song, then… "I've got it. Here's what you're going to do…"

"ARE YOU A MIRAGE?"

"Nope." Sarah grinned when Shane Peters made a show of disconcertedly rubbing his eyes. "Just me."

"Well, *just me,*" he said on the sidewalk in front of Poppy's Antique Emporium, "how'd I get so lucky as to rate more time with you?"

"I don't know," she said with a flirty flutter of her eyelashes, stifling the urge to steal a quick hug. "You must be living right." If Sarah didn't have to keep lying to the man, she'd have told him that she had the next couple hours free now because her brilliant sister had dreamed up an amazing plan.

And if it weren't for her sister's insistence that Sarah maintain the identity charade for the entire weekend, she'd also have told him how much of an effect his probing questions had had on her. Whereas Sarah didn't need even a tiny nudge to want to escape KP duty, ever since the debacle with Greg she had spent an awful lot of her time on work. Too much time.

Crazy as it might seem, something about having made an escape, something more about Shane Peters's smile, made her feel like a giddy schoolgirl—twirling and laughing, with her face tipped to the sun.

"How'd you even find me?" he asked.

Giving him an *oh, please!* look, she said, "Seeing how this block is the only place for about fifty square miles where you can spend an entire afternoon antiquing, it wasn't too hard. Find any of your animals?"

"Not yet, but I have high hopes of Poppy hooking me up." He winked.

And Sarah fell a little deeper under his spell.

"WHAT DO YOU THINK?" she asked an hour later in Past Treasures, trying on yet another funky vintage hat. The pink wool pillbox featured pink-and-white tulle trim, plus what Sarah suspected might be real flamingo feathers.

He sort of smiled. "Nice."

"You really think so? A few of my gal pals and I sometimes wear hats when we go out for Friday-night drinks. I know it sounds goofy, but it's fun."

"The fun factor isn't in dispute," he said. "But in all honesty—and please know this comes from a good place in my heart—that particular model isn't you."

For a millisecond she pouted. But then it dawned on her that she'd just been given an amazing gift, and tears sprang to her eyes.

"I'm sorry," he said. "If you like it that much, maybe you could cut your hair so that it worked better."

"This isn't about the stupid hat," she said, setting it back on the rack. "It's about the way, just now, you were honest with me. I never thought I'd trust another man again. And yet…here you are."

"It's just a hat," he said. "You shouldn't read too much into my opinion."

"I know, but—"

He kissed her. Nothing fancy—at least not on the outside—but what that sweet pressing of his lips against hers did to her insides? *Wow*.

"Sorry," he said, his expression more stunned than apologetic. "I didn't mean to do that. Not that I wouldn't want to kiss you, because I do, but…"

On her tiptoes, she kissed him back. "There. Now we're even." Never mind that her heart was pounding. And that she could hardly breathe.

"*Even* works for me," he said with a devilishly sexy grin. "Now, what were you saying?"

"I'm not sure."

"Wanna start over?"

"In what regard?" Her pulse still racing, Sarah very much wished to start over in *every* regard. Starting with using her real name. She sensed he was such an honest, good soul. What kind of person was she to return his honesty with lie upon lie?

"Like maybe when this weekend's over, we could meet up again. Only not with you as my innkeeper but as friends."

"I can still be your friend *and* innkeeper."

"Oh, I know. But this way I won't feel dirty about it."

"Dirty?" Oh, God. Had he seen dust bunnies, a smudged spoon or a toilet-bowl ring that she'd missed? Sadie was already going to be upset with her for kissing a guest, but if his accommodations had been less than perfect on top of kissing, well, in Sadie's uptight book, there was just no excuse. "What's that supposed to mean? I run a very clean establishment."

"I *know*. All I'm saying is that right now, with me paying you and all to sleep under your roof, something about this whole thing feels a little scandalous."

"Thing—meaning *us?*"

"Exactly. Only there really isn't even an *us* to discuss, you know. More like a *future* us. That is, if you'd want there to be?"

She nodded. Smiled up at him. But her throat was too tight for words.

Oh, she'd love them to have a future, during which they could explore at their leisure the attraction that was brewing between them. Only problem was that once she came clean with him, would he even still speak to her, let alone kiss her?

Chapter Eight

"Make it quick," Hale said over the roar of revving engines. "I've only got ten minutes before the start of my next race."

"It's like this," Heath said from the window seat in his room. "You know Sadie, right?"

"I don't *know her* know her."

"You get what I mean."

"Time's a wastin', bro. What's up?"

"I kissed her, man. And I want to do it again, only—"

"You *what?* Please tell me too many exhaust fumes have me not hearing right. Surely I didn't just hear you say you kissed the woman whose inn I'm supposed to be reviewing. The very much engaged woman I'm supposed to be reviewing."

"She's not getting married. The guy turned out to be a lying bum. Just like Tess—only with *cojones.*"

"If it's true that she's single, I'm happy for you. But seriously, dude, probe a little deeper next week. As for this weekend, she's off-limits, got it?"

"What do you mean *probe deeper?* How much

deeper does it get than going to the source? She told me to my face she broke it off with the guy."

"Again, that's swell, but you made a promise. No fraternizing. Not with Sadie Connelly. This is my career we're talking about. If anyone ever found out we switched, that'd be a hard enough bullet for me to take. But if it also came out that not only did I not do my own review but that the guy portraying me slept with my *reviewee?*" He made a choking sound. "It'd be lights-out for my day job."

"But, Hale," Heath complained, standing up to pace the highly polished maple floor. "I seriously like this woman. If I told her the truth, I'm sure she'd…"

"You so much as hint at the truth with her," Hale warned, "and we're not brothers."

"You look beat," Sarah said when Heath took a stool at the inn's bar. The rest of the inn's ambience was light and airy, but in here, in keeping with the old-world pub theme, the setting was suitably dark and atmospheric. Suiting Heath's mood just fine. A rowdy group of six sat in the far corner, while several couples occupied intimate tables lining the wall. One lone woman had her back to the nearest of three velvet-draped windows. "What's wrong?"

"Nothing," he said, forcing a smile while once again lying through his teeth. Sadie had already been hurt so badly. Sure, at the moment they were just friends, but at the rate he'd been lying to her, once he was finally able to come clean, would she even want to talk to him? "Nothing, that is, that one of your dark beers can't cure."

"Coming right up," she said with a wink.

He took a long swig. "After loafing all afternoon, I figured you'd be elbow-deep in dinner prep. What's up?"

"Hey, I wasn't loafing," she protested, swiping at the counter with a damp rag, "but engaging in guest relations."

"Call it what you want," he said with a teasing grin, "but if I don't get a damn good dinner—" *and a couple dozen more kisses for dessert* "—you'd better believe management's going to hear about it."

"Hear about what?" Mrs. Young wandered up to the bar.

"Sadie here is making a feast. I was, um, just telling her that if dinner tastes as great as lunch, then I'll have to report her to the management."

"But she *is* management, dear."

He and Sarah shared a look.

"Mrs. Young," Sarah asked, "what can I get for you?"

"White Zinfandel, please." Nodding over her shoulder at the crowd, she said in a hushed tone, "Who are all of those people? I was under the impression the inn was quiet and only had six rooms."

"It's very quiet," Sarah assured her, handing her the wine. "Most of these folks are just here for drinks and dinner. Although, as of this afternoon, all six rooms are booked. Four by you regulars," she said with an easy smile, "and one by that couple kissing over there. Then the other by Gretchen Oliver."

"Wonder why she's all alone?" the widow asked. "Mr. Peters, you should go talk to her. Make her feel welcome."

He blanched. Not that he had anything against making

a woman happy, but at the moment only one woman in the room interested him, and that was their hostess.

"Mrs. Young," Sarah said, "the thought is awfully sweet of you, but I'm pretty sure the woman is an undercover reviewer for *Zodor's*."

Heath choked on his latest swig. "Wh-what?"

"Oh, dear," the widow said, patting his back. "Are you okay?"

"F-fine," he croaked.

"Sure?" Sarah asked. "Want some water?"

"No, no," he said, urging her along with her story. "What makes you think she's from *Zodor's?* That's a pretty prestigious publication, isn't it?"

"Only the best inn-and-hotel guide in the country," Mrs. Young said. "Getting five of their coveted silver spoons guarantees an inn's success."

"Really?" Heath said with mock surprise.

"Oh, yes," the widow said. "If the Blueberry Inn were to receive five spoons, our Sadie would be so busy that none of us would ever again be able to speak with her casually like this."

Sarah had now wiped the same spot on the counter for a full thirty seconds.

Understandably, Heath was freaked out by the notion that she thought the mystery woman was from *Zodor's*. But what did *she* have to be upset about? Sure, getting reviewed was stressful, but could there be anything more to her suddenly pensive mood? Did he dare hope the lovely Ms. Sadie was a tad jealous because of the widow's suggestion that he make a new female friend?

"You really think my, um, business would increase that much?" Sarah asked the older woman.

"Absolutely."

"Then I guess I'd better see if anyone else—especially our single new guest—needs a refill."

"Want help?" Heath asked for some unfathomable reason. Maybe guilt? Maybe because she suddenly looked wide-eyed and overwhelmed, and because he, not the mystery woman, was really the person holding the fate of her inn in his hands?

With a light shake of her head, she cast him a faint smile. "You're a dear for asking, but I've got everything under control."

Mrs. Young said, "If you ask me, the best way to ensure a flawless review is with a little romance. Sadie, dear, I know it's none of my business, but accept this young man's offer. Let him help by wooing the lady in question. Not only will she have fun but he will, too. It's a win-win for everyone."

"It's a win-win for everyone," Sarah mocked under her breath. Taking her frustrations out on the poor carrot lodged beneath her butcher knife, she sliced and diced and vowed to give her twin a few of her more pointed thoughts just as soon as she returned.

"Careful," urged Dahlia Sky, the guest chef Sadie had recommended. "You'll bruise their auras."

"Sure. Sorry."

The blond twenty-something chef was supposedly a legend in macrobiotics, and from what Sarah had seen she was doing a pretty amazing job with dinner. But with fresh daisies wound through the four braids that dangled down her back and a pale yellow chef's hat and matching dress, she wasn't exactly the norm. Which was probably the reason Sadie had instructed Sarah to keep the butcher paper over the window as before.

While the chef returned to preparing a Japanese-inspired dish that smelled strongly of ginger, Sarah sulked.

About a number of topics.

Foremost was the undeniable fact that instead of being stuck back here she'd much rather be by Shane's side. Second, for orchestrating a seating arrangement that put Shane alongside Gretchen Oliver—aka Undercover *Zodor's* Reviewer—Mrs. Young was next on Sarah's tongue-lashing list.

She knew the woman meant well and all, but not only was there potential disaster in Shane inadvertently sharing details of his stay that Sarah would rather not have mentioned, what if he actually enjoyed the woman's company? Worse yet, what if Gretchen had done her homework and knew that Sadie was happily engaged? What if she and Shane compared notes?

Head spinning, Sarah tried focusing on the zucchini that Dahlia had asked her to mince, but how could she chop when her head—and Sadie's—were potentially on the chopping block?

She'd already begun formulating an explanation for the weekend's twin switch to Shane. Her plan was to break it to him in stages. First, she'd let him know that Sadie was her twin and then she'd let the whole story unfold naturally. Maybe even add a comic spin. Lord knew, if she heard a friend share this nutty story over a bottle of Chianti, Sarah would find plenty to laugh about.

Being such an honest and caring man, surely Shane would see how Sarah had been forced into this situation. Never would she have willingly lied to him.

Sarah glanced up and caught Dahlia wincing. "Careful. Food is a gift. Our dearest friend. Never should you so callously wound its wholesome goodness."

Scowling, Sarah vowed that when Sadie got back, for having put her through such emotional stress, *she'd* be the one who was wounded!

EYES MOMENTARILY closed, Heath savored the amazing blend of flavors that came with his first bite of Sadie's spring-roll appetizers. Wow, could the woman cook— almost as great as she kissed. Not that their all-too-brief lip-lock had given him a full sample of her talents. Just that, like this predinner treat, the kiss had been a hint of good things to come. Assuming he ever escaped his current companions. To accommodate the extra dinner guests from town, he and the rest of the inn's overnight guests were sharing a table. Mrs. Young had insisted that he and the chatty woman he now dubbed Gabby Gretchen be seated side by side.

This would have been a bad thing had he wanted to talk himself, but since he didn't have much to say that didn't involve Sadie, it was probably just as well he kept his mouth shut. Plus, the downtime gave him plenty of opportunity to formulate just the right tone for the inn's glowing review.

It troubled him that Sadie was visibly shaken by having a reviewer present. If it weren't for the stupid promise he'd made his brother, he'd come clean with her. Assure her that not only would the weekend net her a great review but a great guy. At least he hoped she still thought he was great after he let her in on the little matter of being duped.

"So, Gretchen," the widow said, daintily pressing a green cloth napkin to her lips, "how is it that a lovely woman like you is all alone on a Saturday night?" She spoke so faintly she could barely be heard above the other diners' chatter and the soft classical music.

"Lovers' quarrel," the green-eyed brunette said. The woman was good-looking, but Heath considered himself taken. At least until Sadie learned the truth about him, at which point he'd no doubt be single again. "It's just as well, though. I don't mind being alone. Gives me time to gather my thoughts."

The widow nodded and made a few sympathetic clucking noises.

"You know, though," Mr. Helsing noted, "sometimes the best medicine is a fresh dose of the dog that bit you. Our Shane just happened to have been unlucky in love himself. Told us his date backed out on him at the last minute."

Heath choked on his latest sip of the night's second martini. "Um, with all due respect, I'm sure Gretchen here needs her space. Not that you're not lovely," he tagged on, "just that all this matchmaking has gotten a little out of hand."

"I agree," the brunette said. "Not only that, but Shane's not exactly my type."

"Oh?" Mrs. Standridge said, eyebrows raised. "Do you prefer a more rugged blue-collar sort?"

Hello? Heath wanted to shout. *I'm sitting right here.*

Spring roll poised at her lips, Gretchen said,

"Actually, I can go for either color collar—as long as the collar's attached to a blouse."

Mrs. Young swallowed hard. "Oh." After a few more seconds, her blue eyes widened. *"Ooooooh."*

The subject immediately changed to cruise wear— was it becoming too informal?

Having never been on a cruise, Heath happily munched four more spring rolls. Man, they were good. Someday he'd have to get Sadie to make him a batch of his own.

"Don't you agree, Shane?" asked Mr. Standridge.

"Huh?" He glanced up, only to find all eyes focused on him.

"Haven't you been paying the slightest bit of attention?" Mrs. Helsing released a put-upon sigh.

"I have, ma'am, but the predinner snack is so, uh, *scrumptious* I guess that I lost focus." Probably had something to do with his fantasy of rolling one of those spring rolls along Sadie's flat stomach, then licking off the sweet sauce.

"The gist of it is," Mr. Standridge said with his fingers steepled beneath his chin, "that from a man's point of view, would you be more comfortable wearing a tuxedo or a suit?"

"Oh, a tuxedo. Definitely." Having apparently answered correctly, at least to the older man's way of thinking, left Heath free to return to fantasyland. Now that he'd had a few minutes to think more about Sadie and her bare stomach, blood rushed uncomfortably to another part of his body that seriously had no opinion on tuxedos—unless it involved everyone else in the room hitting the road so that he and Sadie could have the place to themselves. Yeah…she'd fit nicely on top of the table. Wonder if it'd bear his weight, too?

"Mr. Peters," Mrs. Young prodded. "We're waiting."

"I, um…" Heath cleared his throat. Dear Lord, what was he doing? One more mental image like that and he'd have to excuse himself, then run upstairs for a cold shower. "I couldn't agree more."

"With my cruise-ship-surprise-buffet theory as to why the kitchen window's been covered?" Mrs. Standridge asked, eyebrows raised optimistically, as if she stood to win a prize.

"Absolutely," Heath said, shifting to a more comfortable position. "Sounds absolutely plausible."

"I'll bet our Sadie's preparing a magical chocolate forest," Mrs. Young suggested, "complete with deer and squirrel families and a gurgling chocolate stream into which to dip strawberries, bananas and the like."

"Sounds lovely," Mrs. Standridge said, "but highly unlikely, seeing how she'd need more prep space than she's got. After all, I hardly think it likely she'd set up a sumptuous buffet in the kitchen, then expect us to partake there."

The door bumped open, and the same young woman who'd served lunch hustled through bearing a silver platter and a red face.

"I say," Mr. Helsing said, as the teen removed appetizer plates to a side table and then delivered amazingly intricate miniature edible Oriental gardens arranged on square black plates. "Would you mind telling us why the kitchen window has been covered?"

"I really shouldn't," the girl said, nearly knocking over Heath's water in her apparent haste to get away.

Okay. Weird but probably a teen thing.

Choosing to ignore the waitstaff and admire his meal, Heath was blown away all over again by Sadie's culinary skill. Was there no end to what the woman could do?

The mini gardens even had "benches" that were some kind of sushi roll.

Talk about lighting the fuse on what was probably a nonissue, but the teen waitress's refusal to answer had everyone at the table buzzing. Everyone, that is, aside from Heath, who was too busy munching to care about anything else.

For the sake of Hale's review, he supposed he should care, but he knew Sadie. She was the consummate professional. As such, he had complete faith in her to always do the right thing.

"E-EXCUSE ME," SARAH said to Dahlia, more thrilled than ever that her sister had reminded her to recover the kitchen window. "But what exactly are you doing?"

The chef stopped humming and dancing in a tight circle as she gazed skyward—or at least *ceilingward*. "Do you mind? I need solitude during the food-blessing ceremony."

"Oh—so you're just saying a little prayer before dinner?" Sounded reasonable. "You know, like blessing the diners so they have a safe journey home?"

Dahlia shot her a wide-eyed look of incredulity. "It's not the diners who need a prayer but the collective souls of the foods that are about to be eaten. Sacrificed for the nourishment of those who partake."

Speechless, Sarah curtly nodded. Okay. The sooner this night ended, the better.

Two grueling hours later, Sarah had paid Dahlia Sky and sent her on her way. Then she and Coco restored the kitchen's usual order.

"Sure you don't need me to do anything else?" Coco asked, slipping the last of the saucepans back under a gleaming stainless-steel counter.

"Thanks for the offer, sweetie, but you go on ahead. It's been a long day. You've got to be beat."

"Yes, ma'am. But even though it's hard work, it's always fun."

"Really?" Sarah's eyebrows shot up. "You think all this kitchen work and cleaning is actually enjoyable?"

"Sadie says it's a blessing to be able to serve others. You know, to make people happy and content." A wistful look overtaking her expression, the teen added, "When I grow up, I want to be just like Sadie. She's awesome." As if just now getting the gist of what she'd said, she tagged on, "You're awesome, too, Sarah. Just in a different way."

"Gee, thanks." Sarah gave the girl a playful swat with her dishrag, then sent her home. It was cool that Sadie had groupies. She deserved them.

The more Sarah was around this place, the more appreciation she had for her sister. Sadie and her staff worked astonishingly hard to maintain this level of perfection. It was Sarah's fervent prayer that she didn't blow it for all those who believed so deeply in the inn's mission to nurture the spirits of its guests.

Blessedly alone, though laughter could faintly be

heard floating in from the lounge, Sarah drank in a deep breath.

Whew. She still hadn't claimed victory in the weekend-long war, but at least the latest battle had been won.

Or so Sarah hoped.

Surely the reviewer had been pleased by the meal? Chef Dahlia might've been a little *out there,* but she knew what she was doing when it came to edible garden construction! Better yet, the few peeks Sarah had taken into the dining room during dinner had shown her that Shane was as uninterested in Gretchen as she was in him.

Not that Sarah had been jealous of the brunette who was lucky enough to have been seated beside him all evening.

Oh, who was she kidding? Of course she'd been jealous.

If it hadn't been for her promise to Sadie, it could have been Sarah next to him. But now she wasn't sure if she'd ever get the chance to meet him again—for the first time. As herself, instead of her twin.

Seeing how Craig Stevens, the bartender that Sadie hired for her busy Saturday nights, was on duty till midnight, Sarah toyed with the notion of getting away. She'd just get in her car and drive and drive until thoughts of Greg and Sadie and Shane and her worries about how she was going to pull off the preparation of the guests' late-night snacks, let alone breakfast, washed away.

Glancing at her watch, she saw she only had about an hour until she'd need to get started on Sadie's trademark bedtime chocolate-chip cookies. But until then, she'd indulge herself in doing exactly what she wanted to do.

Sort of.

For if she did what she really wanted to, that would include Shane and more kissing. An activity that was strictly off-limits.

Snatching her purse and keys from a hook on the wall, Sarah opened the back door, stepping into the warm, fragrant night. Even as she told herself that escaping the inn would clear her mind of Shane's piercing gaze, his devastatingly sexy grin, his way of making her feel beyond special—as if she were the only woman in the room—she knew it was a lie.

She could run. Hide. Drive all night and into the next day. But even after all of that, one fact would be abundantly clear.

Her burning attraction for Shane Peters was here to stay.

Chapter Nine

In fading daylight, Sarah crunched down the gravel path that led to the detached garage holding her escape vehicle. A black 2003 low-mileage Jag XK8 she'd bought from a client-turned-friend when he'd upgraded to a newer model.

Teeth gritted, she hoisted up the old-fashioned garage door, wishing her twin would spring for a push-button opener.

"Nice ride," said an achingly familiar masculine voice from behind her.

She jumped. "Shane. What're you doing out here?"

"I'd planned on talking to you, but it seems like you have better plans."

"Better than talking to you?" she teased. "What could possibly top that?"

"My thoughts exactly." His expression showed him to be in a playful mood. If only she were allowed to feel the same.

From the forest beyond the lake, an owl hooted. In a neighbor's pasture, a horse softly whinnied. The killer swans must have already bedded down for the night.

"Seriously," he asked, "where are you headed? You look upset."

"How do you know me well enough to judge?"

He shrugged. "Maybe I don't—you tell me."

Unfortunately he'd nailed her pensive frame of mind. With luck, though, he wouldn't realize that the cause of her consternation had only a little to do with the inn and a lot to do with him.

"You're right," she said. "I'm, uh, nervous about the review." Not entirely untrue. Sadie had a lot riding on Gretchen Oliver's opinion. "I've got some downtime and I thought it'd feel good to get out of here for a few minutes. You know, drive out the cobwebs."

"Sounds like a great idea. Mind if I tag along?"

"If you want." Only, *she* didn't want. Did the man have no idea what the mere sight of him did to her? Her stomach tightened with long-denied needs, and her lips tingled from wanting another kiss. Even holding hands with him would be such a welcome experience. Knowing that she was not alone in the world.

Sure, she had Sadie, but her twin was absurdly busy. She led a full life of her own. And Sarah was far too old to be running to her parents anymore.

"Great. Got a destination in mind?"

"Nope," she admitted. "Just away from here."

In the shadows, a mask slipped over his face. Had even that short statement been too revealing in terms of her true thoughts about the inn?

Unable to take back the words, she dismissed them and clicked open the vehicle's automatic locks.

"Nice ride."

"Thanks."

"This afternoon, with you parked at the opposite end of the block, I didn't get a good look, but now I'm thinking we should've taken your car antiquing."

"There's always tomorrow," she said.

"You mean you'd have time?"

"Probably not," she countered. "That was just a figure of speech. But surely sometime I will. Have time, that is." She grinned.

His look was unreadable, so she hedged the awkward moment by climbing in.

Heath followed.

After taking a moment to appreciate the peaceful effect of the sumptuous black leather seats, Sarah reminded herself of who she was and where she was going. This was just one weekend. Come Monday morning, she'd again be the office whiz kid. At ease with her coworkers and the world. Gone would be the bitter taste of her lies to Shane, as well as the awareness of her barely competent handling of her sister's inn.

Slipping the key into the ignition, she fired up the powerful engine.

"It occurs to me," Heath said as Sarah backed out of the garage, then straightened the wheel to glide down the blacktop lane past the house, "that for normally smiling you to be in such a contemplative mood, that the reviewer's presence must be affecting you more than you let on."

"Like I have stage fright?" She shot him a questioning look, hating the way her stomach tightened pleasurably at the view. The sky behind him was awash with orange, and he was a dark enigma in the shadows.

"Exactly. Which I assume was the reasoning behind

you blocking out the kitchen window. Only, seeing how I've now had the pleasure of two nights and a number of meals at your fine establishment, I know you have nothing to fear. Even if you think the kitchen wasn't quite up to your customary level of perfection, I know that if the, uh, woman has half a brain, she'll give you a great review. Meaning, you don't have a thing to worry about."

She laughed. "Oh, but I do." If she blew her sister's chance at that coveted five-spoon rating, Sadie'd roast her for dinner. Thank goodness Shane had assumed the window being covered was simply about vanity, rather than about hiding a substitute chef!

The scenery had changed from pastoral countryside to typical small-town, with a strip mall, convenience store and fast-food sprawl. Heath said, "I didn't realize Winchester was this big."

"You mean this urban, instead of just being quaint?"

"I was trying to be polite."

Sarah also figured that he was trying to change the subject. Bless him. "The actual town is charming, near the antique stores we hit this afternoon. Lots of red brick with lovely old Queen Anne homes and towering oaks. The original drugstore is still open. It used to be quite the hangout in its day. Tons of celebrities have their autographed pictures on the walls. If you get the chance, it's worth a trip for one of their malts or Coke floats. Or just to buy a pack of gum from the counter and soak up the ambience."

"Sounds delicious—gum, malts and atmosphere. Wanna go?"

"You mean like now? This late, they're closed."

"Not this second. Tomorrow. We could make a day of it. Hit a few of the antique stores that we missed today, then have soda-fountain fare for lunch. You can drive." He winked.

"I'd like that." Pulling into the deserted lot of a small park, she turned off the engine. More than he'd ever know, she'd like to go on the date. "But there's that pesky little issue of my professionalism hanging between us. What if that reviewer found out? Even about all the time we've already shared? I mean, I'm no expert, but ethically would it be right for us to hang out even more?"

"Don't have a clue." He sighed and shook his head. "Trouble is, I've got this problem."

"What?" Her pulse was racing again, only this time—to judge by his suddenly "serious" tone—for pleasurable reasons.

"The more I'm with you, the more I want to know you—way beyond what you're serving for the next meal. Trust me, more than anyone, I know how wrong my admitting this must seem. I know, after what you've been through with your ex, you're probably wondering if I come on to every beautiful innkeeper. But please, Sadie, you've got to believe me. What I'm feeling for you is…" A harsh laugh spilled from his lips. "Never mind. I'm treading on dangerous ground and should just—"

"What, Shane?" Sarah couldn't help but ask. "What is it you were about to say?" *Because if it was in any way an admission along the lines of mine—that ever since I first laid eyes on you, I've been unable to get forbidden images of you out of my head—then by all means, go ahead and say it.*

"Only that…" In the last burnished rays of sun, he leaned closer. "In case you didn't know it, not only are you a great cook but you're gorgeous."

"Th-thank you." *So are you, Shane Peters*. Which made the conversation all the more improper in light of certain promises she'd made her twin.

"One more thing—I want to kiss you again. Bad. What do you think?"

"About your urge?" she asked in a voice so low and husky and brimming with the same sudden all-consuming urge that she barely recognized it as her own. "Or about the kiss?"

"Either? Both?" He'd leaned closer still. And so had she. The car's interior was hot. Her crazy attraction for him hotter. Though she knew she was playing with fire even just flirting with the man—especially when back at the inn there was a woman who held her sister's life in her hands—Sarah couldn't help herself.

The guy appealed to her.

Not just with his striking good looks but with the way he'd preserved her sanity.

The whole weekend long, in running her sister's high-maintenance inn, Sarah had felt like a fish out of water. But Shane, with his funny, warm ways, had turned a potential nightmare into a grand adventure. Whether he'd been helping her with a toppling stack of towels or saving her from what had surely been a woman-eating snapping turtle, in a very short time the guy had begun to mean something to her. Even more meaningful was the fact that he'd survived a broken heart, as well, yet had lived not just to tell about it but to thrive. Now relishing the simple pleasures of a day spent fishing and antiquing and, then maybe tomorrow slurping old-fashioned soda-fountain malts.

"I, um…" She licked her lips. "Forgot the question."

"In a roundabout way, I asked if you thought it'd be all right if we kissed."

"Right. Now I remember."

A hint of a smile played across his lips. "Then you think it would be wise? The kiss?"

He leaned closer.

"No," she said in a breathy whisper.

She leaned closer still.

All that remained between their lips was a sliver of supercharged air. A mingling of warm breath. Oh—and those thousands of reasons why they shouldn't kiss, even though it would be so easy and would feel so right.

After what she'd been through with Greg, getting to know Shane better wouldn't be finding just a soft spot to fall but a place to grow. She could learn to feel and laugh and enjoy life again. With Shane, the gaping wound in her heart could finally begin to heal. Above all, Shane was honest—a fact he'd proven that afternoon by something as simple as saving her from buying that goofy, unflattering hat.

"Sorry," he said, pulling back just as she'd been on the verge of lunging forward. "It's obvious that you feel uncomfortable about us being together."

Was it? Because never in her life had she fought such an achy yearning. She wanted *everything* from this man. His kiss. His touch. His friendship. And maybe, just maybe, if he could ever bring himself to forgive her once he'd learned the depths of her lies, they'd one day share so much more.

"What're you thinking?" he asked.

"Truthfully," she said, drumming her fingers against the wheel, "I was just thinking about the past for a minute. And wondering why even though I promised myself I'd never, ever fall fast and hard for another man again, I seem to be doing just that."

"Is that an admission that I'm not the only one fighting this thing between us?"

"You could say that."

"Tell you what." He cupped his big hand against her cheek and she leaned into the touch, meeting his penetrating gaze as she did. "For now, until the inn's reviewed—but more importantly until you feel ready—let's table this. After that, fair warning, Sadie Connelly. Prepare to be wooed."

WHAT THE HELL AM I DOING? Heath couldn't help but think as he unloaded the last of the inn's forks, knives and spoons from a commercial dishwasher. His brother would certainly never help out like this—at least Heath sure didn't think so.

The crotchety overnight gang had been plied with drinks by Sadie's capable bartender, and Sarah was upstairs, doling out late-night liqueurs and warm chocolate-chip cookies Heath had seen her take from the oven, beautifully browned.

What he'd also seen, however, were telltale signs of packaging that made him think the legendary cookies were store-bought. The blue-and-white wrappings had been shoved deep into the trash, and the only reason he'd even found them was that he'd seen the overflowing can and offered to take it out. In the process of tying the bag, the whole thing tipped, spilling trash and secrets.

Now, Heath was all for store-bought baked goods. No way he'd ever bake anything from scratch for himself. But Sadie advertised fresh homemade cookies each night for her guests. He'd sampled them the night before and they'd been delicious. The fact that she'd lied about what should've been—for her, anyway—no big deal, made him wonder.

Clearly, she'd lied. But she'd also gifted him with one of the hottest near kisses he'd ever had.

Tess had been an immediate turn-on for Heath. She'd been wild in bed, which was probably one of the reasons he'd been blindsided by her treachery. And he'd sworn to never again let a woman get under his skin in that way. Tess had been like slow-acting poison—only never had dying felt so good, at least until he'd discovered his prize game design had been sold out from under him.

Fast-forward to the present, and he found himself in the untenable position of being fiercely attracted to Sadie. She was gorgeous, smart, talented and funny, but it troubled him to think this might be one more in a series of chinks in her innkeeper's armor.

There'd been her confusion over getting him registered. Her admission that the inn she supposedly loved felt more like a trap than her life's calling. That odd bit about her not even knowing where the oars were kept. The kitchen window, and now frozen cookie dough. Yet she professed to be one of the most accomplished chefs in Missouri.

If he hadn't offered to help out in the kitchen, he'd have never known about the cookies. He'd have been as oblivious as her guests—and he wished he still was.

His brother never would've even been in the kitchen, except maybe for a couple of impromptu inspections.

So what was Heath supposed to do with this information?

After Sadie finished tucking everyone in for the night, they'd made a date to meet by the lakeside gazebo for more talk—and, Heath had hoped, at least one more kiss. But now he didn't know what to think, other than that if he and Sadie were to have any hope of exploring the chemistry between them, he owed it to himself to confront her about the cookies. He had to know why she'd lied not only to him but to her guests.

"You're a doll for helping me like this," Sarah said, bustling into the room and planting a silver tray on the longer of two stainless-steel counters.

"My pleasure," he said, pulse racing. Was now the time to bring up Cookie-gate? Or should he wait? Until, say, after the weekend was over and he could come clean on a few matters himself. For starters, by telling her his real name.

"Look what I found," she said, wagging a half-full bottle of red wine.

"Is that what goes with cookies and edible Japanese gardens?"

"Beats me," she said, popping the cork, then reaching into a cabinet for two glasses.

"Isn't that sort of thing—wine selection—in your realm of expertise?"

With a wrinkling of her nose, she shook her head. "I only do cookies."

Her statement caused apprehension to ripple through him. The path of least resistance was to let the matter slide. But, looking back on it, he'd also let warning signs slide with Tess, and look where that had landed him. The thought of a master chef like Sadie knowing nothing about wines was ludicrous.

"Look, we need to talk." He cleared his throat, which suddenly felt rather thick.

"Okay…" She took a sip of her wine and then his. "Ready." She grinned, creating a war within him. He barely knew her and yet something about her was magnetic, pulling him in. No matter how many inconsistencies he'd discovered in her behavior, he found himself wanting to move forward. Believing there had to be a logical explanation. One that maybe he wasn't kitchen-savvy enough to have picked up on. "Well?"

Again he was at it with the throat clearing. "You, uh, know how earlier in my stay we talked about our rocky pasts? And how we appreciate truth?"

"Uh-huh…"

"Gimme that," he said, reaching for one of the wineglasses and taking a fortifying sip.

"Why do I get the feeling I'm in trouble?" she asked, her once-bright expression fading.

"You're not in trouble," he said. "I just—for me—need something cleared up."

"Okay, shoot."

"I took out the trash for you and—"

"Thank you." She gave him a one-armed hug, brushing her soft, warm curves against him and making his task that much harder. "Jeez, could you be any sweeter?"

Could you be any tougher to confront? "Here's the thing, Sadie. While taking out the trash, I came across cookie-dough wrappers."

"And?"

"That's it. You advertise homemade fresh-baked cookies every night, yet you just served fakes. What's up with that?"

"It's stuffy in here," she said, topping up both their glasses. "Let's sit outside."

He followed her through the back door and into the scented night. The soft swish of automatic sprinklers on the lawn accompanied crickets, and in the dark forest the hoot owl was doing his thing.

In the gazebo, both of them sitting on thick floral-patterned cushions, Sarah said, "I see where you're coming from on the cookie issue. I hate lies as much as you, but here's the deal. I always keep a few helpful items on hand, in case of an emergency. Say a toilet overflows in one of the guest rooms and the time I would ordinarily take to bake is gobbled up by being a plumber's assistant. Now, would it be better to not give the guests any bedtime snacks? Or tell a harmless white lie so that everyone can go to bed happy?"

"Sorry," he said, hating that he'd turned into the kind of guy who jumped to conclusions. On the flip side, he loved how Sadie's logical explanation set him at ease. "Makes perfect sense. I guess maybe I'm still overreacting to every little thing."

"Don't sweat it," Sarah said. "I totally understand."

More than anything, she wished she hadn't needed
the short walk to the gazebo to gather her confusing
thoughts and come up with a plausible explanation as
to why her truly fantastic chef of a sister *would* need
store-bought cookies. Point of fact, Sadie would
gnaw off her own fingers before she lowered herself
to open a package of cookie dough. But Sarah had
been in a bind and she'd taken the only escape she
could think of.

Sadie, being Sadie, had mixed more than enough
dough to last two whole weeks, let alone one
weekend. But Sarah, being Sarah, had accidentally
knocked the plastic tub off the counter. Not only had
the tub cracked but cookie dough had splatted out the
sides and all over the tile floor. The end result had
been pounds of unsalvageable dough. Meaning that
last night she'd made a mad dash to town for replace-
ment dough.

At the moment—and maybe not ever—she couldn't
tell Shane the true reason for her fib. Because she
loved her twin, Sarah would do anything within her
power to ensure Sadie's happiness and well-being. Too
bad that meant lying like a rug every time her mouth
was open. Her only option, in coming clean with
Shane, was in attempting to explain part of her genuine
past, so that he knew she was sincere in what she felt
for him—whatever that happened to be.

"You sure?" he asked. "That you understand, that is?
I don't mean to be suspicious, it's just that after—"

"Shhh." She pressed her fingers to his lips. "Forget
it. I have."

He took her hand in his, and for the longest time they

just sat there, drinking each other in. He was so strong, capable. His honesty was spellbinding. Which only made her own lies that much harder to bear.

"Despite our earlier agreement to try and control our feelings, may I kiss you?" Heath asked.

Throat tight, Sarah said in a raspy whisper, ignoring her twin's opposition, which was raging through her head, "I've been hoping you would."

"So then I could ditch the whole gentleman routine, go slightly caveman and take what I want?"

"Arghf," she said, trying for a cavegirl grunt and ending up laughing in his arms. And then kissing, glorious kissing. His lips were strong yet pliant, working against hers with a slow, sensuous rhythm. By mutual consent, they took it to the next level with a potent sweep of their tongues.

Heath was the first to draw back, cupping her face in his hands and stroking the apples of her cheeks with his thumbs. "What have you done to me, woman?"

"Funny," she said, pulling back slightly to take his hands, kissing his wrists, "but I was just thinking the same about you."

"Guess that blows the take-our-time-getting-to-know-each-other decision all to hell."

"Yeah." Her single word, whispered hot and moist and sexy as she rested her forehead against his, only made him want her more. "That *was* pretty amazing."

"Ditto."

"So…what do you want to do now?"

"In terms of us?" He stole another kiss.

"Uh-huh. Think we ought to at least try behaving?"

"Probably." He kissed her again. When that wasn't

enough, he slid his splayed fingers under the last remnants of her messy ponytail, urging her closer, deeper.

"Then how come what I'd rather do is take this inside?"

Drawing back and framing her face with his hands, he asked, "You sure?"

Kissing his wrist, she nodded.

"I'm cool with it if you want to end it here—I mean, I'm not," he added with a laugh, "but you know what I mean."

"Uh-huh." She kissed him. "I know exactly what you mean. I also know how much I want to throw away the past year and run as fast as I can toward exploring a future with you."

Her words should have made him feel like a god.

Instead they pushed him deeper into the realm of pond scum. She was too good for him. She'd already been hurt. Why couldn't he regain some semblance of control—at least until he was able to tell her the truth without jeopardizing Hale's job? At which point they'd start from scratch, with nothing but the truth between them.

"It might be better to go slow—for you, I mean." Though nothing could be worse for him. He'd tossed out the suggestion to be polite. If she agreed that they should cool things off, he might quite literally die from wanting.

She shook her head, kissing him again, drowning him in emotions he couldn't label. Never had he wanted a woman more and never had he felt more like a hypocritical bastard about it. He had to cool this down. But how? Why? If she was into him as much as she claimed to be, then she'd understand how he hadn't been able to refuse his brother's request for help.

Right. But was he willing to take the risk of her never speaking to him again if she didn't understand the whole connection? How they'd always been there for each other—no matter what. Heath couldn't expect Sadie to understand the bond, since she wasn't a twin. But he sure as hell wanted her to.

"Your room or mine?" she asked on the heels of a breathy mew.

Lord.

Back to cupping her face, he slid his fingers into the hair at her temples, telling himself he didn't want her quite this bad. Didn't have to have her more than his next breath. But even as he told himself all that, he was tipping her head to get a better, deeper, ever more intimate angle to kiss.

"Yours," he somehow managed to say. "Fewer stairs." More to the point, less space and time for him to change his mind. Less potentially incriminating evidence for her to inadvertently stumble upon. For example, his driver's license and credit cards.

They were back to kissing, meaning he'd realized the time was long gone for backing out, taking the moral high road. He'd already jumped on the express train to hell, and the way it was going, it looked as though he'd enjoy the trip down.

As for the fallout from what happened when Sadie finally met the real him—he'd have to deal with that later. For the moment, he could only handle one crisis at a time. And, God help him, making love to Sadie had become priority one.

Chapter Ten

"I can't wait much longer," Heath said as he stopped midway across the dark dining room, clutching her to him. Sarah had to agree. "How much farther to your room?"

"Through the parlor, past the entry hall, through the game room, past the laundry room, down another hall, through the——"

"No good," he said after another fiery kiss. "What's closer?"

"Storage closet." Taking his hand, she led him that way, yanking open the door and not even bothering with the overhead light.

"Mmm…good thinking," he said, unbuttoning her blouse while continuing to kiss her.

"Hurry," she said, getting their arms in a tangle in her mad rush to remove his starched white button-down. "Oh, my. You're glorious," she murmured, splaying her fingers across the muscular width of his chest. Save for a smattering of rough hair, his skin was warm and smooth. She pressed kisses onto the base of his throat, moving her lips to his shoulder while unbuttoning his fly.

"How can you tell? It's pitch-black in here."

"I just know," she said, hitching her breath when he unfastened her bra, then drew a nipple into his mouth. Her hands at the back of his head, Sarah drew him closer, ignoring the cold bite of stainless-steel shelves against her shoulder blades.

How could something that felt so completely right be so wrong? But seriously, she and Shane—together— could lead to all manner of trouble. Her sister was her best friend. No way could she betray her. Standing here, panting for a man she hardly knew, even though she felt as if she'd always known him, Sarah realized they had to stop. She had to somehow remember she wasn't here as herself but as Sadie.

She shivered.

"Cold?" Ever the gentleman, Heath pulled her shivering body against his.

She nodded, fighting the wall of confusion and frustration and hurt that was crushing her chest. "Um, Shane?"

"Yeah?" he asked in a wary tone.

"I'm sorry, *seriously* sorry, but I can't do this. With that reviewer upstairs—" *and my sister's accusatory glare in mind* "—I just can't."

His breathing ragged in her hair, he chuckled. "I'd be lying if I said I wasn't near death from this development, but I'll recover." And to prove it, he stepped back and fumbled with the buttons of her blouse.

"I am sorry."

He kissed her. Softly. Sweetly. Without a hint of anger, just bittersweet remorse. "No apologies. When the time is right, we'll both know. Until then, we'll cool it."

"Thank you," she said, crushing him in a hug. Yet again this man had proven himself honorable and trustworthy. Yes, chemistry sizzled between them, but their friendship was more important. Which only made the burden of sharing her true identity with him that much harder to handle.

"What's wrong?" he asked, brushing the pads of his thumbs over her cheeks, almost as if through the darkness he could see the change in her mood.

"Nothing," she said.

"Regrets?"

"Dozens. But I do think waiting is for the best." On tiptoe, her hands behind his head again, she pulled him to her for another kiss—the only cure guaranteed to take her mind off her other troubles. Shane just had to understand the whole funky twin thing she shared with Sadie. If it weren't for that there was no way she ever would have conned him like this. If only he were a twin himself, maybe then he could understand the bond. But since he wasn't and would never know the sometimes weighty burden that kind of a relationship created, she could only pray he'd forgive her one day.

Believe her when she told him the truth and then swore that normally she was an honest woman.

COLD WATER BEATING his shoulders, which ached far more from guilt than from having rowed all morning, Heath closed his eyes.

Legs outstretched, palms flat against the shower wall, he fought to make sense of the previous thirty minutes. Maybe more to the point, why he'd been so weak as to ever have let that happen—especially when so much was at stake for his brother. But, no, it wasn't fair to absorb all the blame. It wasn't as if he'd been alone in that closet. Sadie had been a woman possessed, and he'd loved—or at least had wanted to love—every square inch of her.

Trouble was, he hadn't had the right to.

On weekends he might be into extreme sports, but when it came to relationships, he was a rock-solid stand-up guy. A guy who could be trusted. Until now. With the one woman who'd somehow come to mean more to him than all his past lovers combined.

Which was why, when Sadie had seemed in such an all-fired hurry to get away from him after their near miss in the closet, he hadn't objected. He'd blamed her rapid departure on things that didn't matter. Hurt. Inn-related work that had to be done. Having to wash her hair. Any number of tasks his imagination stirred up to ensure her leaving hadn't been personal.

Oh, he didn't for a second believe she hadn't enjoyed their heated kisses as much as he had. What he was starting to fear, however, was that for whatever reason she regretted them. As much as he'd wanted to go all the way, he was glad now they hadn't. She was the kind of woman for whom he'd want their first time to be special. Not such a freight train of desire that he hadn't even seen it coming.

One minute he'd been kissing her, wanting her. The next he'd almost been inside her.

He thumped the heel of his hand against the tile wall. Enough.

They'd stopped in time. His vow to Hale was still intact, and when the weekend was over, maybe, just maybe, he'd get a second chance with Sadie after he'd come clean about his lies.

They'd known each other barely twenty-four hours. It was understandable that after sharing something as mind-blowing as those kisses, she'd need time to process the situation. Lord knew he did.

Cutting the water, he slid open the glass door and reached for a fluffy white towel, thinking about how far out of his element he was. Sadie was the kind of woman who deserved careful wooing—not hot sex in a dark closet.

Oblivious to the lushness of the towel, the bathroom's glowing chrome fittings and pristine white tiles, he dried, then half dressed in jeans and a white shirt. He didn't bother with shoes. The other guests had been tucked in their beds for hours, and so the odds of being seen were next to nil.

Curious not just about Sadie's whereabouts but about her mood, he wandered down the long hall that led toward the inn's public zones, glancing into room after room. Finally finding her by a sliver of light that leaked under the kitchen door.

"There you are," he said softly.

She stood at the counter, wearing loose white pajama bottoms and a skintight white tank. Her long, wet dusty-blond hair spiraled down her back, dampening the tank in spots and giving it a see-through effect that made him instantly hard.

So much for willpower.

One look was all it took to shoot his hands-off

resolve all to hell. Especially the thought that she hadn't been the only one needing a cold shower. "You're gorgeous."

Casting him an over-her-shoulder grin, she laughed. "I'm wearing pajamas—old ones."

"And I must say," he teased, snagging her around her waist to pull her in for a kiss that showed all was still good between them, "you're wearing them especially well." Judging by her smile, his doubts had been groundless. At least for the moment. "Now, what're you doing that was so damned urgent you scurried from our closet hideaway?"

"I was hardly scurrying," she said. "Just wanting to shower, then surprise you."

"So, then, we're good?"

"Yeah," she said with a blinding smile. "We're better than good. At least we will be once we finish snacking and get to bed."

"Bed?" With spiked eyebrows, he said, "Wanton woman."

"Let me rephrase that. Once we snack, then hit *separate* beds."

"Ouch." Crooked index finger to his mouth, he bit. "Sadie Connelly, you're a heartbreaker."

She landed a light smack against his abs. "And you're incorrigible."

SEATED CROSS-LEGGED on Sadie's rose-colored floral explosion of a four-poster bed, Sarah shoved a cheese cube into her mouth to keep from wanting to press her lips all over Heath's bare chest.

Though one of her favorite movies was playing—

Animal House, which coincidentally was one of his faves, as well—there wasn't a whole lot of watching going on.

They'd talked about everything under the sun. Their passions, pet peeves, political views. And when they'd finished talking, she'd snuggled against him, wanting nothing more than to be with him in every sense of the word. But along with the crushing want came paralyzing guilt. And, again, Sadie's disapproving face.

Sarah wished she'd could tell him everything—highlighting the most important parts. Like how she wanted to kiss him and hold him but wasn't allowed to. Did he think her strange? Prudish? "Shane?"

"Uh-huh?"

"Back in the closet, did you think I wasn't attracted to you?"

He laughed. "Hon, the way blood was rushing to certain parts of my anatomy, I wasn't thinking of anything other than keeping you in my arms."

"Yeah, but—"

"Shh." He silenced her with another kiss. "Not another word. We agreed to take things slow, and I'm okay with that."

"Promise?"

"Sort of." He winked.

Exhausted from the day's adventures, she yawned and then laughed. "Sorry. That was in no way a reflection of how I feel about my company."

"Sure. I can tell when a woman's bored with me. Lucky for you, you won't be for long." Tackling her, pinning her to the mattress, he was ruthless in his tickling.

Laughing so hard that she snorted, she fought back,

but she was no match for his superior strength and tickling skills.

"I can't wait to get you to my place in St. Louis."

"Oh, yeah?" Sitting up on her elbows, she grinned. "What's so great about it?"

Fingering strands of her hair, he said, "I've got a penthouse with floor-to-ceiling windows and a view of the whole world. One of these days, I want to explore you there—every inch of you. I want to erase every trace of heartache you've been through. I want to—"

"Thank you," she managed to say past the sudden knot in her throat. "But you've already done so much. With you, I have this incredible sense of having been reborn. Like I've been granted a cosmic makeover, and this time I'll get the whole relationship thing right." She'd get all of that, that is, assuming Shane forgave her lies.

And if he didn't?

The question consumed her with a melancholy terror. How could she have just found this one-in-a-million guy, only to lose him on a technicality?

Cuddling against him, she was suddenly exhausted. "Shane?"

"Hmm?"

"Would you spend the night here? In my room? Just holding me?"

"It would be my pleasure. Especially since you've got to be up fixing me a delicious meal in less than five hours."

"Excuse me?" Was he nuts?

"Hey, you were the one who told me you have to rise with the roosters to start breakfast and prep for lunch and dinner."

"Ugh," she groaned. "See what you've done to me?" *You've got me so mixed up inside, I've somehow managed to forget who it is I'm trying to be.* Which led her to the inescapable and awful fact that during all the excitement over hiding her nutty nighttime guest chef, Sarah had forgotten to arrange for breakfast help.

She hadn't even called Helga to see if she'd be back in time to help with lunch. Meaning, unless the Cooking Fairy appeared during the night to land a magical conk on Sarah's head, the Blueberry Inn's guests could look forward to the only breakfast food Sarah expertly prepared.

Pop-Tarts.

WHEN SADIE'S ALARM pealed at five o'clock Heath was loath to wake her. Never had he seen a woman look sweeter in her sleep. Everything that had gone wrong in his life before seemed to have been erased. As if one amazing night with Sadie had somehow set him free.

Yet, in reality, he'd never been more aware of his personal demons. All due to the role he'd taken on as a simple favor. A lark he'd not seen as having consequences. Sadie would get her five silver spoons. His brother would keep his prestigious job and at the same time ace his races. The weekend was to have been a win-win situation for everyone involved.

So what'd happened? Where had he gone wrong?

Gazing at the angel beside him, looking ethereal in moonlight, he traced his finger along her cheek. "Wake up, Sleeping Beauty."

With a groan, she rolled over, taking the down comforter with her.

"Hey," he complained, tugging back the covers. "What kind of hostess are you? Freezing out your guests?"

"You know," she said, her voice husky and sexy with sleep, "I could turn that around and ask what kind of guest you are, to be in here harassing your hostess at such an ungodly hour."

"The pain." He clutched his chest. "I hate getting shot down before the sun even rises."

"Speaking of rising," she said as she rolled over in bed, "I guess I'd better get with the program."

"What's on the menu?" he asked, hoping it was something really delicious like the blueberry pancakes his brother had told him was a signature dish. "I'm starving. Some wild woman kept me up past my bedtime."

"So now it's all my fault?" she teased, straddling him and tickling his ribs.

"Damn straight." Kind of like his latest growing *problem,* which was caused by having her ride him as if he were her own personal stud. Hands on her hips, he hitched her lower until she sat directly atop his most problematic area. "See what you've done?"

"I did all that?" she asked, her eyebrows innocently raised as she ground against him with an erotic sway of hips that said she not only knew what havoc she was raising but that she was having a good time doing it. "Promise, I didn't mean to."

"The hell you didn't," he said with an affectionate growl, reaching for the hem of her thin white tank and stopping just short of slipping his hands up, up, up, until they cupped her full breasts. In his mind, the heat of his palms tempted her nipples to come out and play. If he had the morning his way, he'd make love to her thoroughly, then serve her breakfast in bed, giving her a much-deserved break. "Now you'll have to be punished."

Arching her head back, she closed her eyes and dazzled him with a not nearly sated female smile. "Sounds good to me. Only trouble is I've got serious KP duty."

"Rats, and here I was hoping to start the morning off with this…" He tipped her forward, whispering plans in her ear that had nothing to do with cooking but plenty to do with satisfying hunger.

IN THE SUN-FILLED dining room, after he'd surveyed his leaning stack of pancakes, Mr. Standridge tossed his napkin to the table and then said to the woman everyone assumed was a reviewer, "Have you ever eaten anything more abysmal?"

Gretchen blanched. "It is *interesting*."

Seeing how Heath was busy gulping iced tea in an attempt to wash down his latest bite of pancake, which had a texture somewhere between concrete and egg yolk, it took him a second to leap to their hostess's defense. "It's not *that* bad."

Liar!

The last thing he'd expected after Sadie had urged him to relax and catch up on his sleep while she fixed breakfast was a culinary disaster. He'd offered to help, but she'd refused. What if, in keeping her up all night, he was the cause of this disgusting glop? Granted, it looked good, but the taste… Yech.

Leaving him with an even bigger problem than his attraction to her. How would this meal affect the review of the inn? If he was honest, he'd have to acknowledge the unpalatable fare. But the part of him that was fiercely attracted to her told him to let the incident slide.

Sadie was tired.

She shouldn't be expected to cook.

"Personally," Mrs. Young said, "this meal strikes me as very odd. Does our Sadie have a split personality when it comes to the kitchen?"

"Has anyone noticed the bacon?" Mrs. Helsing piped in, plucking a strip from her plate and giving it a wag. "It's both undercooked and burned."

"Shh…" Mrs. Young said. "Everyone quiet. She's coming."

"I couldn't care less," Mrs. Standridge said. "We paid a pretty penny for this weekend and…"

"She's trying awfully hard," Heath said in a hushed tone. Maybe the widow's warning had been a false alarm, but nonetheless he didn't want Sadie to overhear the less-than-flattering conversation—especially since it must be in large part due to him. "We should give her a break. Or, for that matter, maybe we could all pitch in and cook a little something. I do some mean scrambled eggs. Mrs. Young? I'll bet you've cooked a few biscuits in your day."

"That I have."

"Are you listening to yourself?" Mrs. Helsing hissed. "We've all paid good money to be pampered. Have meals cooked *for* us. And here you sit, proposing we cook for ourselves?"

Heath's stomach sank.

The woman was hard to take, but she was right.

His suggestion of storming the kitchen to prepare

their own meal was ludicrous. If Hale had been seated in his place, he'd ream out poor Sadie, whereas Heath longed to jump to her defense.

Trouble was, the only reason he was even at the Blueberry Inn this weekend was because he was playing a role crucial to his brother's professional survival. Hale was depending on him. And what had Heath done? Gone and fallen for the very woman he'd promised to impartially critique. But was it fair to trash her cooking when he was to blame?

"In, uh, passing yesterday," he said, "I learned Sadie's been short-staffed the entire weekend. As such, I'm thinking we can't really expect her to keep up her customary perfectionist's routine."

"What I think," the widow said, "is that you've taken a fancy to our Sadie."

"That would explain your leaping to her defense," Mrs. Helsing added.

Both Standridges nodded their heads.

Mr. Helsing was back at work on his pancakes.

Gretchen focused on the fruit salad, which was fairly harmless.

Heath raked his fingers through his hair, wishing himself anywhere on the planet other than this room with this particular set of overindulged busybodies.

"Anyone still hungry?" Sadie asked, bursting in on the scene carrying a tray loaded with turnovers and cinnamon rolls, a bright smile lighting her olive eyes.

"Never stopped being hungry," Mr. Standridge grumbled, lunging for one of the tray's treats. He took a swift bite, chewed, then shocked them all by actually smiling in apparent satisfaction.

Following his lead, the Helsings helped themselves, as did Mrs. Young. Heath took one, too, but— dammit—from the first delicious bite, he knew full well Sadie had unfortunately had nothing to do with this latest addition to their meal.

Chapter Eleven

"Good?" Sadie asked in respect to Heath's latest bite, looking every bit the proper innkeeper in her starched khakis, white blouse and frilly pink apron. She wore her long hair pulled neatly back, with a minimum of makeup. In short, she looked fresh, beautiful and completely in charge of her world.

Only, he knew she wasn't, because he prepared identical-tasting refrigerated rolls for himself at least a couple Sunday mornings each month. As she had the night before, over the cookies, once again Sadie was lying. Sure, she was short-staffed, meaning she might not have had any choice but to resort to store-bought baked goods. But enough was enough. Surely the woman had backup support she could call upon?

While he brooded, and the bamboozled guests oohed and aahed over their sweet pastries, Sadie retreated to the kitchen all smiles.

Pleased another near crisis had been averted?

Heath wished he could say the same.

With everything in him, he wanted to trust Sadie. Believe the only reason she was turning out such forgettable fare was because the woman she falsely believed to be a reviewer had distracted her or made her nervous. Better yet, believe she was exhausted from being up most of the night with him. But was that the real cause? Could Hale have somehow been wrong in his belief that Sadie was a master chef? How? Even the *Zodor's* executive editors thought Sadie to be a gourmet goddess. How could so many people be wrong? Hell, if Heath didn't know better, he'd swear he wasn't even dealing with the same person.

With satisfied guests wandering off to their rooms, the garden or the game room, media room or library, Heath couldn't stop himself from moseying into the kitchen.

"Need help?" he asked.

She stood at the sink, washing heirloom china by hand. "Thanks, but I've about got it handled. Plus, Coco should be here any minute. What I don't finish, she can tackle."

He nodded before hefting himself up to sit on one of the empty steel counters.

"I don't think the health department would like seeing you up there. Although maybe later, after my current guests leave and my new ones have yet to arrive…" She winked.

He glanced over his shoulder. "Mmm, I like where that thought's leading. Aside from the inspector bit. Please tell me you're not expecting one soon?"

"Nope. Just my reviewer in there." Apparently in a playful mood, blissfully unaware of just how upset her guests had been over the awful pancakes, she pitched a dishcloth his way. It landed on the nonslip tile floor a good five feet from his comfortable perch.

"Missed," he taunted.

"Hmm…" Drying the last plate with a fresh cloth and then wiping her hands, she said, "Seems to me back in grade school there was a rhyme to that effect. Something to the tune of *Missed me, missed me, now you've gotta kiss me.*"

"That could be arranged." Hopping down from the counter, he snatched the rag.

"You wish." With a flirty smile and a flip of her ponytail, she sashayed out the back door into brilliant spring sun.

"You're a tease, huh?" He followed her, wishing he had the willpower to go straight to his room to work on the write-up of the inn's disastrous breakfast.

"Maybe…" She tilted her face back, drinking in the sun, and said, "Have you ever seen such a gorgeous day?"

From where he stood, it wasn't the day that commanded his attention. More like her formfitting white blouse and hip-hugging khakis, which were doing little to stop his memory from running wild with images still fresh from their intimate night. In the soft morning light, her complexion was flawless, save for a smattering of freckles across her nose—to him, more asset than flaw. And then there were those eyes.

Then something, maybe the scent of fresh-watered mint growing in the garden, reminded him of his brother, who was forever chewing mint gum. Heath preferred Juicy Fruit. Kind of the way he preferred juicy-looking women, fully rounded and lush like the dream girl who was worshipping the sun before him.

Trouble was, Heath was here to do a job and not find a girl. Hell, in his wildest dreams—for the foreseeable future, at least—he'd have never imagined himself looking for anything other than a one-night stand. But with Sadie there was a kinship he couldn't resist.

"You know how you're all the time asking to help?" she said.

"Why do I have the feeling all that asking was a mistake?"

"Oh, now," she sassed, landing an elbow to his ribs. "Where's your sense of adventure?"

"Depends. Are we talking about more dishes?"

"SEE?" SARAH ASKED Heath an hour later at the farmers' market set up around the town's square. "Is this so bad?" One glance at the man who was laden with paper sacks bearing zucchini and tomatoes and berries and she burst out laughing. "Stupid question, huh?"

"I've had worse days—spent digging ditches."

"Do that often, do you?" In the dappled shade of a red maple, she paused before a fresh flower stand. The only blooms she recognized were daisies, but the rest were pretty and fragrant and would be perfect for that afternoon's table settings. Even better, maybe for once she'd actually look as if she knew what she was doing. The more she was with this man, the more she wanted to not only please him but impress him with her innkeeping prowess.

Fat chance, seeing how the closest she'd ever come to flower arranging was picking all their neighbor's tulips on Mother's Day when she and her sister were ten, and her sister had shown her up by giving their mom a perfect heart-shaped clay ashtray. Didn't matter that their mom didn't smoke. The thing had been gorgeous—

just like everything Sadie touched. Like her perfect decorating and cooking and her relationship with Trevor.
Sarah adored her sister, but just once she would've liked
to have a smattering of those domestic skills and luck
with men for herself.

"Me? Dig ditches?" Heath said with a deadpan expression. "Every chance I get. How else do you think
I got these guns?" Setting his bags on a bench, he
pulled back his short-sleeved red polo, brandishing a
bicep that she remembered all too well.

"Impressive," she said with a whistle, wishing her
true feelings didn't mirror the first word out of her
mouth. The man was delicious. Both bare-chested and
in clothes. Now, if she could serve *him* up for dinner—
say, back at her St. Louis condo, along with a couple
of restaurant-takeout steaks… That was her true defi-
nition of *fine cuisine.*

"What brought on that enigmatic smile?" he asked,
back in pack-mule mode as he picked up his bags to
head to the next stall.

"Wish I could tell you, but it's strictly confidential."

"In that case, I'm afraid I'll have to insist you tell
me or else…"

"Or else what?" she asked over her shoulder, telling
herself—not very convincingly—that he wasn't the
hottest man she'd ever seen.

"I'll go on strike."

"Leaving me to carry all this on my own?"

He shrugged. "You're the one calling the shots."

"All right, suppose I explain what brought on that
smile? What do I get in return?"

"Let's see… I could offer to take you to lunch, but

seeing how you're due back at the inn, I suppose that's out."

"Yep." If only he knew how tempting that offer truly was. Especially seeing that how she'd only just barely recovered from breakfast. At least a quick call to Helga had been rewarding: *Bubbka* was feeling much better, and that was why Sarah had needed to rush to the market. To fill Helga's grocery list. Even better, the cleaning staff was already hard at work on the rooms, and Coco would be in by noon to help with the lunch service. Meaning the rest of the day should be an easy coast until Sadie got home. "What else you got to deal with, mister?"

"There's always cash," he said with a hopeful grin.

"Nope. The inn's crazy popular." At least it would continue to be if she could rein in her attraction sufficiently to keep her sister act afloat. With a reviewer on the premises, it was more important than ever that Sarah maintain a convincing front.

"Okay," he said with a sigh. "Well, I guess that only leaves one option."

"And that would be?" Was it a bad sign that the closer he came, paper bags crinkling between them, the more turned on she was? The more her heart pounded, dying for another kiss. So much for her plan to ditch the attraction. Let's face it—when it came to denying herself Shane Peters, she was as hopeless as she would have been attempting to prepare the meal Helga had planned for lunch.

Good thing there was a Sonic drive-in nearby, because in the event Helga bailed at the last minute, Sarah wouldn't have enough willpower to give up kissing simply in order to cook.

"THIS HAS BEEN FUN," Heath said on the way back to the inn from the passenger side of Sarah's car. "Do this often?"

"Um, all the time. Freshest ingredients make the best meals."

"What's on the menu today?"

"It's a surprise."

He nodded, praying that whatever she prepared for lunch would turn out a damn sight better than those leaden pancakes. Fighting a fresh round of guilt for having kept her up late the night before and feeling honor-bound to at least try to do a good job for his brother, Heath cleared his throat and asked, "What happened with breakfast?"

"What do you mean?" Her hasty glance away from the road looked stricken. "Everyone seemed to enjoy their meals."

"Yeah, well…"

"Shane? What do you know that I don't?" Deep concern shone in every nuance of her face. Instantly, for even bringing up the subject, he felt about as loyal to her as a bag of dirt.

What about your twin? his conscience scoffed. *Remember him? The guy you've been intimately acquainted with for all but the past couple days of your life?*

"Shane? Come on, tell me."

"Sadie, hon." He reached for her free hand, giving her a squeeze. "You know I adore you, right?"

"Oh, no. I have a bad feeling about what's coming next. Shane—" She swerved off the road into an abandoned service station lot. With the engine softly idling, she said, "Please, tell me you think the reviewer's not giving the inn less than five spoons. I mean, if you think there's even the slightest chance she wasn't completely satisfied with her meal, I need to talk to her. Explain that if there's anything she's experienced this weekend that she might've found less than exemplary, it's not normal. Usually this place is run with blow-your-mind efficiency."

"So—and please don't take this wrong—what's happened this weekend that's out of the ordinary?" He brushed her wrist with her thumb. "Because in isolated spots, you seem nothing like the woman that dozens of glowing recommendations describe you as."

"I've tried." Her sniffle broke his heart. "I've really, *really* tried. Everyone seemed satisfied with breakfast. What did you think was wrong?"

Everything! "Well… Not to be overly critical, but the pancakes were a smidge tough."

"Tough?"

"Yeah. But," he lied through the same teeth those tough-as-leather discs had damn near cracked, "just a smidge."

"What else was wrong? Because the plates looked beautiful. I made all those orange peel and cherry garnishes and—" Tears streamed down her cheeks.

"Don't cry," he said, unfastening his seat belt and then hers, to awkwardly pull her into his arms.

"It's just that a great review means so much, especially from *Zodor's*. I've been out of my mind with worry over whether or not their reviewer would show. And then last night, when she finally checked in, I tried so hard to impress her. Sure, I was tired this morning, but not enough so that I didn't feel capable of doing my best." Inching back from him, she wrung her hands on her lap.

The same hands that hours earlier had skimmed along his chest. Wasting time she probably should have spent in the kitchen, instead of allowing him to monopolize her, er, talents.

Silent tears flowed.

"Oh, hon…" Could he be a bigger ass for even bringing up the subject? Of course her pancakes had been awful, but he was entirely to blame. Any sane person—especially a sane *guy*—would agree. "No more tears, okay? Of course you're getting five spoons. The pancakes weren't *that* bad, and if I hadn't hogged all your time this morning, I'm sure there never even would've been an issue. I'd bet big bucks that woman from *Zodor's* has been thrilled with everything you've prepared."

"Uh-huh," she said with a sniffling nod. "So you really don't think she'll hold breakfast against me?"

"Not a chance." And as for the store-bought rolls, *he'd* ignore those, too.

"Thank you," she said before launching into a fresh batch of tears.

"Now what's wrong?"

"N-nothing," she mumbled. "I'm just so relieved. You have no idea the kind of stress I've been under with that woman here."

"Look," he said, softly brushing back her hair from her forehead. "You have to know I never in my wildest dreams imagined this weekend would turn out the way it has. I'm sorry if my being here and wanting to spend time with you has interrupted your ability to work."

She nodded, and as he lowered his hand, cupping her cheek, she leaned into his touch.

"At best, I figured on walking away with a few extra pounds from your great cooking. At worst, a mild case of indigestion. What I got is…" He lowered his hand again to reach for hers, interlocking their fingers. "Pretty amazing."

"I agree," she said. "And now that the review will finally be done, maybe I can take some time off. Get to know you without the inn's constant pressures hanging over my head."

"That's a nice thought, but how are you going to have time later? Especially when all those silver spoons have the potential to double your business?"

"I, um…" She bowed her head. "I'll figure something out." Glancing away from him, nibbling her lower lip, she added, "It probably won't be as hard as you think. And what about you? With you working so much, getting together could be rough."

"I, uh, wouldn't worry about it," he said. "You're the real problem—what with you being so tied down."

"Tell you what," she said, casting him a brilliant smile and then taking back her hand to swipe at the few tears that remained. "For the moment, let's not dwell on problems but on tons of future possibilities."

"Great plan." He kissed her. Kissed her with all the hope that was swelling in him for that bright future she so loved to discuss. The same future that, when he thought about coming clean with her as to his true identity, made Heath queasy as hell.

"I TOLD YOU," MRS. YOUNG said, fork poised at her grinning mouth. For their last meal of the long weekend, all the guests shared one large, elegantly dressed round table. "Our Sadie has split cooking personalities. Now tell me, Gretchen, have you ever in your life tasted *carré d'agneau à la provençale* done more divinely?"

"It's fantastic," the brunette agreed, as did the rest of the crew.

"Mr. Peters?" the widow probed. "What do you think? Have you ever tasted a better dish?"

"No, ma'am." Especially since he wasn't even quite sure what the woman had just said.

"And the *gratin d'épinards aux champignons* is an exceptional accompaniment," said Mrs. Standridge, apparently not to be outdone by the widow's lavish praise.

"Mr. Peters?" the widow asked again. "What do you think?"

"Uh-huh." Especially since now he wasn't quite sure what *either* woman had said. The only thing that mattered was that all three gals seemed pleased. As did the men. *Whew.*

The tasty meal came as a huge relief after having already, in a sense, promised Sadie her spoons. Now that he knew without a doubt the threat of being reviewed—plus his own distraction—was the sole cause of her cooking anxiety, he could rest easy, knowing his brother's reputation would be safe. The Blueberry Inn would receive the highest rating.

"Don't you find it odd, though," Mrs. Helsing asked, "that one meal is to die for and the next can be less than perfect?"

"In all our travels," Mrs. Standridge said, "I've never seen anything quite like it. The especially curious thing is that when our hostess shines, it's to such a wondrous degree. I find myself not even caring what happened with the previous meal."

"Well said," murmured her husband. "Shall we all meet here again next year, in the hopes our hostess has worked out her few remaining kinks?"

At the word *kink,* Heath nearly choked on his latest mouthful. How many different ways had he imagined he and Sadie would one day make love? A coughing streak left him fighting for air.

Mrs. Young thumped his back. "Are you all right, Mr. Peters? Are you breathing?"

Sort of.

He nodded. "I—I'm good."

"That's a relief. Ours wouldn't be much in the way of last-day celebrations if we were to lose a fellow traveler."

The general consensus was that everyone was relieved he was alive. More specifically, if Heath had to hazard a guess primarily they were relieved to not have an interruption to their meal.

"Not to change the subject," Mrs. Helsing said, "but have any of you been fortunate enough to see the Broadway production of *The Lion King?* I was just talking to my daughter this morning and she…"

Thrilled to have the spotlight off him—which was to say, off his brother—Heath used his navy napkin to wipe sweat from his upper lip. Would this gig ever end?

Yeah, but then what? How would he begin to tell Sadie the truth? After what'd happened to him before, he'd sworn no relationship he entered into would be less than one hundred percent honest. Yet what was he doing?

Sadie was a wonderful woman. He owed her so much better than the half-truths she was currently getting.

So why not come clean with her now? Why not storm the kitchen, drag her out to the gazebo or up to his room and tell her everything? Never under ordinary circumstances would he have played such a dirty trick. But his twin brother had been in a bind and—

No. He couldn't come clean with her now, because if her fury happened to make its way to Hale's boss, his brother could be fired. No matter how badly Heath's gut churned with guilt, he had to stay mum as to his true identity a while longer—at least until Sadie was in a great mood because of her awesome five-spoons review. After that, maybe she'd view the switch as funny—and not deceitful at all.

Chapter Twelve

"Your lunch was incredible."

"Thanks." Though Sarah eagerly stepped into Heath's outstretched arms, basking in the glow of the compliment, his kind words did little to ease the tension that knotted her shoulders. They were blessedly alone in the dining room—at least for the moment. Helga and Coco were still in the kitchen, cleaning up. Which was probably where she should be, too, but she couldn't tear herself away from him. Not quite yet. Not since it'd occurred to her that in a few hours, on the off chance Sadie returned before he departed, there'd be some major explaining to do.

"Oh," he said with a relaxed laugh, "trust me, after that meal, I'm the one owing you thanks. I don't know how you put that together in such a short time, but I'm in awe. Your five spoons are well deserved."

Not really, but whew. At least the inn's reputation was intact. As for her personal life after telling Shane the truth…

"What's wrong?" he asked. "You seem down."

"Just tired," she said. Which, along with a few

dozen other issues, happened to be the truth. Afraid of being caught by the reviewer in Shane's hold, Sarah stepped back, putting her hands to her forehead. "No offense, but I'll be glad when this weekend's over."

"I don't blame you. But you know, I was thinking… Seeing how back in St. Louis I'm the boss and there's really nothing pressing I have to be back for, how about we take tonight to—"

On her tiptoes, she stopped him short of asking if he could stay the night. If this had truly been her inn, she'd have suggested he stay the week, but with her sister due home soon, the party was *waaay* over. "Don't get me wrong—I'd love nothing better than for you to hang out longer, but…"

His eyes narrowed. "There something you're not telling me?"

"Like what?" A nervous giggle escaped.

"Oh, say, like everything we've shared was fun but ultimately a mistake? One you're now trying to graciously extricate yourself from?"

"No way," she said, hands to his chest, stealing another kiss. "Trust me, this has nothing to do with you and everything with me. My, um, sister's due any minute for a visit, and—"

"Why didn't you tell me? I'd love meeting her."

"Any other time, that'd be great, but…" She glanced over her shoulder, then lowered her voice. "She's going through a really bad time. Um, man troubles. She's coming here to avoid any and all men and basically spend her week trashing anything with a penis, so you can see where this might not be the best time for you to meet. Especially with me being so blissfully happy."

"Seriously?" he asked.

"About the penises?"

"No," he said with a playful growl, tugging her back into his arms. "About you being blissful."

"Of course I was serious about that. In case the past forty-eight hours didn't give you the message, I'm just as stunned by what's happened between us as you are. But along with that, I'm ecstatic—and so much looking forward to spending every spare second getting to know you better. Just not next week."

"Understood. And not a problem," he said, nuzzling her neck. "But once your sister leaves, I'll be back. Often. And then—"

"No." So he couldn't see the stricken look on her face, she gave him an ultratight hug, hiding her horrified expression against his chest. "Let me come to you. I've been dying for time away from here. Plus, we can go to the zoo." *Where we'll both be nice and relaxed and in a public place, so there won't be much yelling when I break the truth to you.* It was odd not even knowing what Shane was like when he was upset, but she did know the biggies. Like he was the most kind, caring and sexy man ever. Not knowing his every personality quirk was exciting. Like something to look forward to. A big present to slowly unwrap.

"Oo-kay." His flat expression was unreadable.

"Great," she said with forced cheerfulness. "Then it's settled. Next weekend's at your place."

Cupping her cheeks, tilting her gaze to meet his, he asked, "Why do I get the feeling you don't want me here?"

"Oh, no." Kiss, kiss. "I—I can see how it might look

that way, but you have to know nothing could be further from the truth. I adore you. Can't wait to spend more time with you. It's just that—"

"At the moment, the timing couldn't be more wrong?"

"Exactly. So you understand?"

"Totally. Come here." Hand on the back of her head, he urged her lips to his, telling her not with words but with feeling how much he truly did understand. Which should have made her feel better. For today at least—shoot, for the whole week—she was home free.

Sure, but what then?

How would she break it to Shane that most of what he thought he knew about her was a lie? What if he was the domestic type who enjoyed plenty of home-cooked meals? What if he was attracted to that in her? Or, rather, Sadie? What if he hated driven corporate types like the person Sarah actually was? What if once he learned the truth, he never spoke to her again?

"I DON'T WANT YOU TO GO," Sarah said a short while later that afternoon, sitting cross-legged on the foot of Shane's bed, watching him pack. On her head was the long-billed fishing cap he'd loaned her during their time on the lake.

There were no doubt a cajillion inn-related tasks that needed completing, a million more details having to do with her own packing. Yet here she sat, yearning for a few more stolen minutes with this man who, if only she could find the courage to tell him the truth, she could see again tonight. She had a St. Louis condo. They could order takeout and rent movies or talk or go to a park and just stroll holding hands. They could do all of that, that is, if right now, this very second, she told him the truth. Honesty was always the best policy, and if she was straight with him before Sadie even got here, surely he'd see she'd never meant him harm.

Heart pounding, palms sweating, she took a deep breath. "Shane, I—"

"Sadie, I'll stay if you want me to. All you have to do is say the word and I'm yours." He leaned over to kiss her with such tender urgency she couldn't ruin the moment.

Even if it means saving what could be your only shot at sharing a future?

"I want you to stay," she said. "I really, *really* do."

"But…" He kissed the top of her head, then returned to his overnight bag, tossing in a paperback that looked as if he'd never even cracked the spine. "Don't worry about it. I understand about your sister and I'll be back ASAP."

"I know, it's just that…" Her eyes misted. Never having thought of herself as the crying type, yet at it again, she brushed at her tears with the backs of her hands.

"Hey," he said softly, cradling her cheeks, making her feel alive and tingly and one hundred percent female in the way only he ever had. "I'm a phone call away. Or if you've changed your mind and you think your sister can handle being around me without causing certain—" he cleared his throat "—necessary body parts harm, then I'll be happy to stay. Otherwise…"

The pregnant pause said it all.

Otherwise he needed to get on with packing.

She needed to suck it up and let him go.

"You'll probably need this," she said, slipping off his hat.

"Keep it." He pressed a butterfly-soft kiss onto the tip of her nose. "It looks way better on you."

Throat aching, she nodded.

"Smile for me, okay? It's not like I'm heading off to war—just St. Louis."

"It has bad neighborhoods."

"Granted, but not anywhere near my place."

"Promise?"

He nodded before landing the sweetest kiss to her lips. "I'm heading out," he said. "You stay here. Take a nap before your sister arrives. After all the work you've done this weekend, you deserve a break." With one last squeeze to her shoulders, one last fleeting kiss, he opened the door, then gently closed it, leaving her feeling more alone than ever.

Hugging herself, giving in to the tears she felt as if she'd held at bay her entire life, Sarah snuggled back into the king-size canopy bed. Shane had only been in it for two nights, and yet it still smelled of him. Clean and masculine and good.

Shane.

The man she somehow, some way had grown to love already. Impossible but true.

Next weekend, once she'd broken the truth to Sadie, she'd tell Shane. Until then, she'd indulge in that nap, dreaming of their reunion. When there'd be no more secrets between them. Only a love she prayed he felt strongly enough to be able to forgive.

CLIMBING FROM THE passenger side of her Land Rover, Sadie called over her shoulder to Trevor, "Sweetie, would you please feed the swans? I'm worried that Sarah may have forgotten, and it looks like she never found the gardener's number." Shaking her head, she added, "I knew I should've called him Friday morning before we left."

"Give it a rest," Trevor said, stepping up behind her to cup her shoulders. The air in the garage was stuffy. Thick with a mingling of scents from the grainy swan feed to the faint smell of gas used to fuel the weed-eater and the riding mower—both items she kept on hand in case of shaggy lawn emergencies such as this. "The guy was celebrating his anniversary. If he couldn't turn up at his regular time, what makes you think he'd have wanted to do it this weekend? Babe, relax. The place looks great. I'm sure that the reviewer loved it."

"I know," she said, stomach fisting as she suddenly felt unbearably tense. The weekend had been long and strange, and it was good to be home. Home, where she could think. Breathe. "If she saw fit to grant five of her silver spoons, my every worry will be over." At least her every *business* worry. As for personal matters, Trevor had yet to set a date for their wedding. Would he ever?

"Now that you've redone the garage," Trevor said, "where'd you put the overgrown-goose grub?"

"Right there." She pointed to the large plastic tub alongside the immaculately boxed Christmas lights. In her daily life, she was the very embodiment of organizational perfection. Why, then, did her personal life feel like a shambles?

"Found it," Trevor said. "Go on. I've got this handled.

I'm hardly a Farmer Ted kind of guy, but I can see how antsy you are to discover what shape the inn is in."

"Hey," she teased, kissing him, "this is going to be your place, too, one of these days."

"That's right," he said, kissing her back. "Assuming, that is, I ever find a place in my busy schedule to make it official?"

"I wasn't going to say anything, but…"

Kissing her again, he said, "I've put a lot of time into thinking about this subject, and it occurred to me that I've always been a kid at heart."

"Yes…" Her heart pounded.

"As such, what would you think of a Christmas wedding?"

"You mean it? There'd be an awful lot to do between now and then. Putting a proper wedding together takes time. I'd have to stockpile baked goods and—"

"Lord, help me," he said on the heels of a groan, tugging her into a hug. "I love you, but as tight a ship as you run, this place'll be the death of me."

"Hopefully not till you're a hundred or so."

"God willing," he whispered into her hair. "That sounds just about right."

Behind them, a swan hissed.

Laughing, they parted.

Heels of her hands to her suddenly stinging eyes, she flashed the man she loved a brilliant smile, took a moment to compose herself, then tossed back her long blond hair and snatched her rose floral overnight bag.

A Christmas wedding. Perfect.

"Looks like I'd better get to feeding your brood."

"Thank you, Trevor."

"It's no big deal."

"I don't mean the swans."

"I know." For a long time they stood there, gazes locked. "Thank you, too, Sadie, for putting up with me for all this time. I can't wait to marry you. I'm just sorry it took me so long to finally reach that conclusion."

While Trevor went off to feed the swans, Sadie ambled toward the inn. The place that wasn't just her livelihood but her lifeblood. With Trevor by her side as her husband, the future shone incredibly bright.

With him at the lake, Sadie aimed for the back porch, about to burst with happiness and dying to share the news with her twin. Her wonderful, perfect, fabulous twin whose help had allowed her and Trevor this much-needed time, which had obviously helped him make a decision about their wedding.

She'd just reached the herb garden when a man called out. "Sadie?"

Glancing over her shoulder, she saw a good-looking stranger charging her way across the blacktop lot and then the lawn. He'd left a leather bag alongside a black Jeep, and in his hand he carried a small white paper bag.

"Hon," he said with enough shaded emotion in his voice to infer they were best friends—or more. "I thought you were inside?"

"I—I was just headed that way," she said, "but who are you? How do you know my—"

Marching straight up to her, he kissed her fast and hard and in such a blazingly intimate way that her long engaged heart stormed with guilt.

"Damn, I'm going to miss you."

Fingers to lips that were raw with confusion, Sadie

had just processed the fact that this rogue kisser must've mistaken her for her sister—her apparently misbehaved sister—when from out of nowhere Trevor appeared.

As luck would have it, the stranger still held her in his arms.

"Let her go," her fiancé railed, yanking her free. "Who do you think you are, just walking up to a woman and—"

"Sadie?" Heath asked, unfazed by the Nordic Neanderthal's rough touch yet devastated at the thought he'd apparently been duped by the second woman he'd loved. Yes, it sounded crazy even to him, but somehow during the depressingly brief weekend he had grown to love this woman.

"I'm sorry," she said. "Apparently there's been a misunderstanding."

"You think?" Mind and heart spinning, he urged, "Sadie, please. Talk to me."

Staring, she shook her head, her look not one of returned love but of pity.

He wasn't remotely afraid of a fight, but he was terrified of losing her forever before she'd ever truly been his. Hale had been right. She was engaged. Dammit, how could she have done this to him? Talked with him. Laughed with him. Kissed him, when the whole time she'd been promised to another man? What the hell had he been to her? Some kind of twisted game?

Slow-burning fury clenched his fists.

Oh, he knew her game all right. Even as her fiancé hustled her across the lawn toward the house, Heath muttered under his breath on the way to his car, "You're a fantastic actress, Sadie. All along you played me for a fool."

And to think he'd been worried about his comparatively insignificant lies to her. Lies that hadn't especially hurt anyone but rather had helped.

Damn Sadie Connelly to everlasting hell.

Damn her to the degree she'd eternally damned him for falling in love with her.

Chapter Thirteen

What was the commotion outside? Were the
Standridges carrying on again?

Clutching Shane's hat to her chest, Sarah scooted
from the bed to go to the window, parting lace curtains
to peer outside.

No.

The word shuddered through her, as did the horror
of having seen Sadie, Trevor and Shane together. No,
no, no. Fate wouldn't be so cruel.

She was on the verge of chasing after him to explain
whatever interpretation he had of what he'd seen, when
from down the hall came serious clomping. "Sarah?
Sarah, you up here?"

"I'm here," she said, her voice raspy from too
many tears.

Oh, boy, time for the crap to hit the fan.

"There you are," her twin said, practically running
into the room. "Good grief, I've looked everywhere for
you. You'll never believe what happened to me just
now—or maybe, seeing how you've obviously gone

against my wishes and…" Her eyes narrowed as she rounded the foot of the bed. "Sarah?"

"Uh-huh?"

"Why did a man I've never met kiss me like we were lovers? Did you…?"

"No." But she'd wanted to make love with Shane, assuming that's what Sadie was implying.

"Sarah…" Her twin's voice was lethally low. "Please don't tell me that instead of impressing my guests—the *Zodor's* reviewer, for heaven's sake— you've been up here indulging in some fling?"

"I could tell you that," Sarah said, nibbling her lower lip, "but, um, it wouldn't be one hundred percent true."

"Oh, God." Her twin did a melodramatic flop onto the rumpled bed. "Let me get this straight. Not only did you ignore the reviewer but you launched a relationship with this guy—as me?"

Gnawing her lower lip, Sarah fought for just the right words but found none. Finally she said, "Look, if anyone's seriously hurt here, it's me. I know that reviewer was important to you, and your guests were, too, but Shane's come to mean more to me than the outcome of your stupid review."

"Excuse me, but my livelihood isn't stupid. I've worked years to build my reputation. So help me, if you've in any way affected either my own or my inn's integrity with this stunt, I'll—"

"You'll what?" Sarah fought, straightening to her full height, which unfortunately was the same as her adversary's. "Didn't you hear me? I *love* him. Shane Peters is the one and only man who's ever been able to make me forget what happened between me and Greg. Trust me, I thought—Shane and I both thought—long and hard about even kissing. But—"

"Stop." In a move straight out of fourth grade, Sadie covered her ears with her hands. "I can't stand hearing his name anymore. Thanks to you, I could be ruined. Where is the reviewer? Is she still here?"

"Huh? Sadie, I—"

"Listen, what's done is done. I'll sort it out in the morning. I hope."

Oh, sure, Sadie'd sort out the mess with the inn, but what was Sarah supposed to do about the mess in her heart?

"HEY, BRO," HALE BROWN said, strolling into his twin's office, which looked more like a cross between a fast-food joint and a video arcade. Red-and-black checkered carpet formed an eye-popping foundation for sumptuous black leather sofas and chairs, along with a freakish array of full-size pinball machines and video games. What his twin, Heath, lacked in charm, he more than made up for in cold, hard cash and awesome toys. "How're they hangin'?"

"Shriveled and to the left," his brother mumbled, quoting a line from one of their favorite Jim Carrey movies, *Liar, Liar*.

"Damn. That inn not live up to expectations?"

"Oh, trust me, I got *waaay* more than I'd ever in my wildest dreams expected. Try the hottest kisses ever. Then turning me into the biggest fool when I found the sex-kitten proprietress not only with another guy but wearing his ring."

"Back up." Hale staggered into a deep chair.

Scratching his head, he said, "I told you Sadie's engaged. If you didn't believe me, then it's your own fault."

"She told me they broke up."

"She obviously lied."

"No joke."

With a deep sigh, Hale rubbed his eyes. "The bit about her long-standing engagement was even in her bio. Didn't you read it?"

"Why would I? You told me this weekend was going to be a cakewalk. You told me all I'd have to do was eat, sleep and chat."

"Right. That's exactly what you were *supposed* to have done. So would you mind going back over that kissing part?"

"What can I say, man? She was hot." But beyond that, she was so much more—at least Sadie had seemed to be before he'd discovered her true mission, which was playing him for a fool.

Rubbing his face with his hands, Heath's twin sighed. "You know this puts me in a hellacious bind? Obviously your take on the place is going to be skewed."

"Sorry. It's not like I did it on purpose. I thought we'd made a connection, but apparently the only thing the woman was interested in was getting some kind of sick revenge on all of manhood. And trust me, judging by her acting skills, she'd have stopped at nothing to get it. Oh, and she can't cook, either. I'd planned on overlooking this, but the more I think about it, the more I'm certain she didn't make a damn thing all weekend."

"Bro…" Face scrunched, his brother said, "I see where you'd be upset, but one thing's for sure—Sadie

Connelly is a master chef. She needs no help when it comes to wowing guests with her culinary skills. That in mind, what possible reason would she have to dupe you in the kitchen? Let alone the bedroom? I mean, seriously, you're a good-looking guy and all, but none of this makes sense."

Heath, holding firm to his fury, kept his mouth pressed shut. Fine. Hale didn't want to believe him, so be it. But as far as he was concerned, Sadie deserved the most scathing review ever written in *Zodor's* one-hundred-year history.

Tapping his chin with his index finger, Hale said, "This is voodoo." Standing, pacing, he asked, "Tell me specifics. How was Sadie a bad cook?"

Heath shrugged. "Hard to say. Her debut meal was so-so. One of the guests commented that it tasted like a TV dinner. Sadie's next couple meals were heaven on a plate."

"And after that?"

"Disaster again. She made blueberry pancakes that tasted like chewy blue sponges."

"Whoa. She messed up her trademark pancakes?"

"Yeah. They were awful. Why?"

"Give me a minute." Hale marched to Heath's computer, then typed the inn's Web address. When the home page popped up, showcasing the place in all its sun-drenched glory, Sadie smiling from the front porch steps, he called his brother over. "Come here. I want you to verify something. This is the woman who ran the inn, correct?"

"Duh. Who else would it have been?"

Hale reached for a pen, tapping it against the

desk. "And you say there were times this woman couldn't cook?"

"Depends. Do you think a master chef would use store-bought cookie dough?"

"Now I know something's not right. Those cookies are another thing she's famous for." Hoping to find some clue as to what might've transpired, Hale clicked the mouse onto the Meet Our Staff page. Clicking on Sadie's smiling picture, he was redirected to another screen, this time with not one Sadie but two. "I'll be damned…"

"What?" Heath leaned over him.

"Get a load of this." He tapped the flat-screen monitor. "Brother, I do believe we've fallen victim to our own game. I'd bet my shiny new racing trophy that you weren't with Sadie this weekend but with her twin, Sarah."

SARAH WAS WILING AWAY her Monday by moping on a window seat in the gorgeous lavender Maya Angelou-themed suite that had been designed for poets and lovers, not scowling singles. She should've gone home to lick her wounds. The elegant floral wall-paper was doing nothing to improve her mood. Nor was the tricked-out white marble bathroom with its whirlpool tub for two. And while she was on the subject, the king-size lace confection of a canopy bed sucked, as well. As for the lavender potpourri Sadie insisted was supposed to brighten her mood—don't get her started.

So why was she here? Using a vacation day that would have been better spent in Tahiti? Simple. Sadie's cooking was so good it was almost medicinal. As an added benefit to hiding out in Winchester, she could mope in relative anonymity. The last thing she needed on top of a broken heart was a bunch of girlfriends telling her what she already knew: that she'd been foolish to fall for a guy so fast—*again*.

In a way, the fact that she and Shane appeared to be at the end of their brief fling was for the best.

Sarah had known all along that no good could come from having lied about so many details of her life, but throughout the past weekend she'd prayed Shane would be the understanding type. That he'd see her switch with Sadie not as deceitful but as more of a lark.

Now she snorted at the likelihood that Shane, who'd made it clear how much he despised liars, would take a sudden shine to a woman who'd pretended to be someone else. And judging by the way he'd stormed off Sunday afternoon, it must not have occurred to him that she could be a twin.

Determined not to waste her free time feeling miserable, but instead, getting past this bump—okay, this crater—in her personal road, she pushed herself up from the window seat, checked her hair in the mirror, then headed down to help her sister in the kitchen. Based on her less-than-stellar culinary track record the odds were good that she'd soon be kicked out. But, hey, at least then she'd be close to the inn's library and she could grab a good murder mystery.

She'd just dragged herself down the stairs and into the entry hall when the bell over the front door jangled. She glanced that way, expecting to see one of her sister's new guests.

Wrong.

What she did see stole her breath and what precious little remained of her sanity.

"No," she said, hand over her heart. "No way." Standing in the inn's open door, backlit by the late-afternoon sun, was not one Shane Peters but two.

Chapter Fourteen

"Which one are you?" the nearest Shane asked.

Notching her chin higher, Sarah retorted, "Which one are you?"

The guy *chuckled? Her* guy?

Why was it that even when she felt she'd been wronged that her heart swelled at the ridiculous notion all might still be forgiven? Why did she even care, seeing how she'd never forgive him for having pulled the same stunt on her that she'd pulled on him? Whomever he was!

Crossing to meet her at the base of the stairs, the man extended his hand for her to shake. "Pardon my rudeness. I'm Hale Brown." Gesturing to the man behind him, he said, "This is my brother, Heath."

Heath? "Who's *Shane Peters?* Are you triplets?"

The man calling himself Hale winced. "I'm afraid Shane's my alter ego. He's a, um, character of sorts I use to maintain my anonymity."

"Anonymity?" Sarah all but shrieked. "From what? *For* what? What kind of sick games have you two been playing?"

"Funny you should mention game-playing," he said, rubbing his stubbled jaw. "You see…"

"Sarah? Oh, I…" From out of the dining room Sadie emerged, and upon seeing the two men, she nearly tilted backward from the force of putting on her brakes. "I wasn't aware we had company. Which one of you kissed me in front of my fiancé? My still peeved fiancé?"

The man who'd been introduced as Heath said in a bitter tone, "That would be me."

The man who'd tried to shake Sarah's hand said, "As for why my brother made a reservation under an assumed name—my assumed name—that would be because as a reviewer for *Zodor's,* it would be—"

"What?" both Sarah and her twin said in unison.

"B-but I thought Gretchen was the reviewer?" Sadie said to Sarah.

"I thought she was," Sarah replied. Slowly turning to the man she'd thought she loved, she said, "And yet all the time it was *you* doing the review? How could you?"

"And how could *you?*" Sadie asked Hale. "*Zodor's* is a world-renowned publication. You have a reputation for giving the most thorough, comprehensive reviews. Yet you had the audacity, the gall, to saddle my inn with someone who might not have known the difference between a sandwich and a soufflé?"

"Hey!" Heath interjected. "I'm not that dumb when it comes to food. Besides which, any fool could see Sarah here can't cook her way out of a paper bag."

"E-excuse me?" Sarah said. "You told me you loved my food. Was even that just another of your lies?"

"You and I need to talk," Hale said to Sadie. "Preferably somewhere quiet. Away from these two—

who somehow managed to foil both of our ill-conceived plans."

Raising her chin, Sadie asked, "How do you know I even had a plan?"

"Oh, come on," he said with a sarcastic snort. "As a fellow twin, cut the BS. Let's you and I get down to business. Namely, giving your inn the excellent review I still suspect it deserves."

Once her sister and Hale had left them alone, Sarah clung to the stair banister so hard that her knuckles turned white. Almost biting a hole in her lower lip, she launched a desperate search for the right thing to say, to do. Less than twenty-four hours earlier she'd nearly been naked in this man's arms, no secrets between them—aside from hers—but now…

Seeing how she hadn't even known his name, he was pretty well a stranger in every sense of the word. Sort of. If she didn't count the fact that she felt as if she knew every inch of his body. Just nothing when it came to his soul.

"After all we shared," she finally said, "how could you not even tell me your real name?"

He cleared his throat. Looked everywhere else, but wouldn't return her freezing stare. Was it her imagination or had the temperature dropped a good twenty degrees?

"Well?" she demanded, hands on her hips. "Don't you have anything to say for yourself?"

His slow, sarcastic round of applause spoke volumes. "Talk about the pot calling the kettle black. I poured my heart out to you. You knew what I'd been through with Tess, and yet obviously you didn't care."

"And you *did* care about what Greg put me through?

Did it bother you enough to make you even think about telling me your true name? Or the whole time we were together were you laughing inside, thinking it hilarious that once again I was getting played for a fool?"

At the top of the stairs a guest room door creaked open. "Do you mind?" a professorial-looking type with horn-rimmed glasses and a bushy goatee asked, a thick leather-bound book in hand.

"Sorry." Sarah cringed and shot her mystery man a glare. "We'll take our conversation outside."

Storming past Heath, out the front door and toward the gazebo, all she could focus on was how acutely uncomfortable she felt with the man hot on her heels.

"As my brother already told you, my name's Heath. And don't you dare act all high and mighty when I had real feelings for you."

Had?

"Dammit, woman." He gripped her arms, turning her to face him and then giving her a gentle shake. "I thought everything about you was perfection. Then, of course, your sister came home, and I realized all those times I'd wondered about your skills you really *had* been clueless in the kitchen."

"Don't you dare say a word about my cooking, when you heard me go on and on about how nervous I was about the inn being reviewed and all the time *you* were doing the reviewing. I made private, heartfelt confessions to you, and—"

"Oh, right, confessions like how the inn made you feel trapped? Saturday afternoon I even bought you this because the color reminded me of your eyes and how sad you'd looked talking about being tied down." He handed her the paper bag that held her tissue-wrapped necklace and earring set and then he laughed. "That's rich, seeing how it's not even your inn! What other supposedly *heartfelt* confessions were lies?"

Shoving the small bag into her jeans pocket, it took every ounce of Sarah's willpower not to slap Heath. "Yes, I'm a lousy chef. And, yes, everything that could go wrong with the inn did go wrong. But what the two of us shared was real. I adored you. For the record, I'm sorry for having deceived you. It was never planned. It just…happened. And now, for you to stand here and accuse me of…" The pain of it hurt too much to allow Sarah to continue.

First Greg and now this.

How could fate be so cruel?

Heath stood there in the burning afternoon sun, listening to those damn swans carry on down by the lake and pretending Sarah's obviously well-rehearsed speech didn't cut to his core. Even though he knew what kind of lies she'd told, his fingertips ached from the effort of not reaching out to her. Of not pulling her hard against him, massaging away her pain. Hell, the pain they both felt. He was hurting, too. Worse than he'd ever imagined possible.

What if the tears he'd assumed were solely for effect were genuine?

Right. He'd assumed as much about Tess, and look where that'd left him. She'd not only stolen a fortune from his business, but she'd transformed him into the hard-nosed cynic he was today.

"You know," Sarah said, visibly trembling and issuing a runny-nosed laugh, "the whole time we were together, I felt guilty for not coming clean with you. And now I see how misplaced all that negativity was. You're obviously not worthy of the guilt."

A muscle popping in his jaw, Heath asked, "How do you figure that?"

"Simple. In order for me to feel sorry for hurting someone, I need to believe they're human enough to feel pain. You, Mr. Heath Brown, are obviously so far evolved that not only do you not recognize sincerity but you don't even want it.

"Impressive," he said with a whistle, glancing off toward the lake. "Almost as if you've been practicing that line for a while."

"You're impossible," she said, storming away from him and heading back toward the house.

"Oh, that's good—run away. Real mature."

"Don't you dare talk to me about maturity," she called over her shoulder, fury flashing from her green eyes. "I, at least, admitted I was wrong. You, on the other hand, have just stood there looking all high and mighty while assigning blame. But before you get too deep into your own self-pity, you might look in the mirror. Because from where I'm standing, there's more than enough blame to go around."

"What's wrong with you?"

"Wrong with *me?*" From the passenger side of his brother's red Jeep, bulleting down eastbound I-44, Heath laughed. "I'm good."

His twin snorted. "Which must be why you haven't said more than two words this whole ride home?"

A semi whizzed by, thankfully—at least for the

moment—occupying Hale's attention. Allowing Heath a moment to wallow in the misery that filled his head.

Where did Sarah get off talking to him like that? Just like Tess, she'd played him for a fool, and this time he wasn't taking it. He might've fallen for her smooth lines once, but it would never happen again.

"You know she seriously loves you?"

"Huh?" Heath glanced his brother's way.

"Sadie's sister? Your Sarah?"

"She's not mine," Heath bristled.

"Yeah, well, regardless, according to her sister, Sarah fell for you—hard."

"Her loss." Dying a thousand deaths inside, Heath swallowed the knot in his throat. How could the woman lie to her own twin? Had she no conscience?

"Not that it's my business," his brother rightfully pointed out, "but why are you being such a jerk about all this? Just like we were conning them, they were conning us." He chuckled. "Kind of funny if you think about it."

The hell it was funny!

Oh, sure, Hale could sit there laughing, but he wasn't the one who was torn up inside. He wasn't the one who'd opened himself emotionally only to discover the woman he thought he loved hadn't existed outside his mind. The Sadie he'd met had been some odd amalgam, a cross between her homemaking sister and a woman whose profession he didn't even know.

"I'M BETTER OFF WITHOUT him," Sarah said Wednesday night, serving herself another heaping scoop of Sadie's homemade blueberry ice cream. It'd only been an hour since she'd helped Sadie and Helga clean up after dinner, but for some reason she was ravenous again.

The necklace and earrings Heath had given her were safely, secretly tucked in her pocket. The vintage crystals were gorgeous—an exact match to her eyes. How could a man who'd known her such a short time recall a detail like that?

"You keep up this pace, you'll turn into a blueberry," Sadie said, snatching the ice cream tub and snapping on the lid. "Although it might be good advertising. I could make a special curved bench for you on the front porch. Sell tickets so that little kids could come and stare at you."

After swallowing her latest bite, Sarah stuck out her tongue.

Helga bustled in from the dining room. "I tell her that man no good."

Gaping, Sarah said, "*You* were the one throwing us together. Telling me, 'Relax. Go ahead and spend time with him.' Your *eye* said we were a perfect pair."

"You must not have understand. I said no to that man." Tapping her forehead, she added, "Yes, I have the all-seeing eye, and if you would have listened, it said he was no good. *Bubbka* agrees." Helga snatched her battered brown purse and a sweater, then gave both Sarah and Sadie hugs before humming her way out the back door.

Sarah said, "You do know that woman's nuts, don't you?"

"She means well."

"In Nuttyville."

"Seriously, sweetie—" her twin curved her fingers around her forearm "—I'm worried about you. And in her own way, so is Helga. According to Hale, Heath's crazy about you. Literally. The man's reportedly worse off than you. Hasn't been to his office since Monday."

"And?"

"I take this as a clear sign he's being pigheaded and that eventually he'll come around."

"Just in time for a double Christmas wedding?"

Smoothing her hand along the stainless-steel counter, her sister's expression turned wistful. "Wouldn't that be the ultimate in dreamy?"

Laughing, Sarah said, "Oh, it'd be the ultimate in something. No doubt something of a disaster."

"Stop," Sadie said. "Trust me, any day now Heath will realize what a fool he's been and he'll come begging you to take him back."

"What if I don't want him back? He said horrible things."

"According to Hale, Heath's been put through the ringer when it comes to romance."

"And I haven't? And since when are you and this Hale so chummy?"

"Since we both care about our respective twins. Sweetie, I know Greg put you through hell, but maybe you've had longer to adjust. Plus, I guess Heath lost not only his heart but a huge amount of money—which might've worsened the blow."

"I know," Sarah said on her way to the cracker cabinet, fishing out a box of Wheat Thins.

"As an upstanding member of the Royal Order of Cookie Thieves," Sadie softly said, "I have to ask, is there anything I can do to make you feel better?"

"Thanks, but no. I can handle this on my own."

Can you? her conscience nagged.

Could she somehow forget the smell of him? The taste? The way he'd made her feel whole. The silly way she didn't want to try on the necklace he'd given her unless he was the one slipping it around her neck, brushing the tender skin with the backs of his fingers, giving her pleasurable chills while kissing the sensitive spot behind her right ear. She didn't know if she could forget all of that or not. But for sanity's sake, she was sure as heck going to try.

THURSDAY AFTERNOON, when a knock sounded on Sarah's open office door, she looked up, expecting her next client. The last person she'd expected was Heath. At least she thought the man in front of her was Heath. Wasn't he?

"Hey," he said, standing in the doorway, hands in his pockets. He wore sharply creased black slacks and a cobalt button-down that made him even more handsome than usual.

"Yes?" she asked, hoping she came across as cool and unaffected even though her heart felt perilously near to beating right out of her chest.

"Do you have a second? I'd like to talk."

Had he always had that faint scar on his chin? They'd been so intimate. How could she not have noticed?

"Sarah?"

She tensed. The man's words had stung. Hard. Maybe she didn't want to talk to anyone ever again. "I thought we'd said all that we had to say?"

He swallowed hard, gestured to her ivory leather guest chair. "May I?"

"If you'd like."

"You're not going to make this easy, are you?"

"Should I?"

"Honestly? No." After a sad laugh, he leaned forward, resting his elbows on his knees. Fingers steepled, he set his chin on them and sighed. "I said some bad things to you, Sarah. Made completely unfair accusations. And for that I'm sorry."

"Th-thank you."

He nodded. Flashed a faint smile that in her heart of hearts looked nothing like the one she'd thought she remembered so well. Could that be another sign she'd never really known him at all? "Not that it excuses my actions, but falling for Tess, a woman who stole almost everything I had and was…" He patted his chest. "It changed me. I'm no longer happy-go-lucky like Hale."

"Did anyone say you had to be?" Sarah longed to reach out to him, soothe the battered lines around his eyes.

"Anyway." He cleared his throat, pushed to his feet. "That's all I had to say. I just thought, at the very least, I owed you the same apology you gave me."

"Okay." She stood, too, holding out her hand, wishing for a hug but settling for a brief kiss of their palms.

What had happened between them?

At the inn they'd talked for hours, and yet now it felt as if they'd become strangers.

"Take care," he said, releasing her hand as abruptly as he'd taken it.

"You, too," she said past an ache the size of New Hampshire in her throat. So this was it? They wouldn't be bitter enemies, but he no longer wanted to discuss that future they'd been so excited to launch?

With one last lingering look, he was gone.

And inside, where it mattered, a piece of her disappeared. God help her, but she loved him. Maybe now, after having been given that gentle glimpse of his humanity, even more so. He was human, suffering. Just as she was. Only maybe worse, seeing how he apparently refused to release the pain in order to make room for love.

Could she help him find his heart?

Probably, but her gut instinct was that he first needed time to help himself.

WAITING CURBSIDE IN front of her sister's mirrored high-rise office building, Sadie switched the AC higher in Hale's Jeep. He'd left her the keys, in the event his mission took longer than expected. Which apparently it had.

Sadie had told Trevor all about the situation, and although at first he'd been furious at seeing her in another man's arms, he now saw the humor in it—and also sympathized with Sarah and Heath.

Sadie felt awful about meddling in her sister's life, but considering the fact that neither Sarah nor Heath would've found themselves in this predicament if it hadn't been for Sadie and Hale and their misguided schemes, it was the least she could do.

Wiping sweating palms on the thighs of her navy jogging suit, she checked her watch for what felt like the tenth time since Hale had headed for Sarah's office. Would Sarah buy his acting job? When it was Sadie's turn to play Sarah, would Heath take the bait?

"Glad that's over," Hale said a few minutes later, hopping into the driver's side.

"So?" Sadie asked, angling on the seat to face him. "How'd it go?"

"I think all right." Leaning his head against the seat back, he sharply exhaled. "A couple times I caught her eyeing me funny. Like she was sizing me up—comparing me with her memory of Heath. But once I apologized, then launched into Heath's sad saga, she was back in love—or at the very least, lust."

"You *think?*"

He winked. "I know."

"Hope you're right." Digging in her purse for Sarah's favorite shade of lipstick, Sadie pulled down the sun visor to peek in the mirror. With her hair styled like her twin's and wearing one of Sarah's favorite outfits for a weekend of hanging out, she prayed she'd pull this off.

Sarah had been through so much with Greg that Sadie felt honor-bound to see that her sister had a proper chance to find out if Heath was the man for her. If, after this gentle nudge from the people who loved them most, the couple stuck with their decision to call it quits, so be it.

At least Sadie would know she'd tried.

Chapter Fifteen

Late Thursday afternoon in his office at home, Heath had gotten himself so deeply befuddled with his latest game's code he feared he might never find his way out. Sounded familiar. Like a certain relationship he'd recently entered into.

Leaning back in his desk chair, rubbing his stinging eyes with the heels of his hands, he couldn't help but wonder what had possessed him to go off like that with Sarah. While he knew in his head what she'd done was no worse than the stunt he and Hale had pulled, he couldn't work past the feeling that since she'd lied she was essentially no better than Tess.

Which Heath knew was ludicrous. Right?

Gazing around his penthouse apartment with its floor-to-ceiling St. Louis views, it occurred to him that it had been a very long time since the place had felt like home. When he'd moved in two years earlier, he hadn't had time to mess with the settling in himself, so he'd hired someone else to handle everything. On the advice of his brother, he'd found a decorator to do away with all of his ragtag bachelor furniture and replace it with futuristic primary-colored leather sofas and original art, along with plenty of chrome, stainless steel and glass.

Architectural Digest had done a feature on it, so he knew it was a nice enough space, but four thousand square feet on top of the world was too much for one guy to handle. He wanted more. A wife and kids to share it with. He'd moved downtown to be close to all the things he loved. Including Busch Stadium, where he held season tickets for every Cardinals home game.

Up from his desk, roving into the living room, where he paced before a stunning view of Gateway Arch, he prayed for a sign. Something to tell him Sarah was the right girl for him.

But then he'd known Tess for over a year before he'd declared himself in love with her and yet he'd never truly known her. He'd sort of known Sarah for a weekend and still he felt as if he'd *always* known her. That his life had never been complete until he'd held her in his arms. Sappy as hell, but there you had it.

He owed her an apology, but at this point—after the immature name-calling he'd indulged in—would she even agree to be in the same room with him? Let alone be gracious enough to listen while he stumbled through some sort of an explanation, when really he had none.

What was there to say other than he was sorry? That if she'd give him another chance he'd—

The doorbell rang.

He sighed.

The last thing he needed was Hale showing up again, urging him to give Sarah a call. *If* he called her, it'd be on his own terms. When he decided he was mature enough to stop comparing Sarah's every action to what Tess had done.

The doorbell rang again.

Figuring Hale wouldn't leave without having his say, Heath yanked open the door only to get a shock. Instead of confronting his brother's goony grin, there was Sarah, stone-faced and yet more gorgeous than ever.

Mouth dry, he looked to his feet. "How'd you know where I live?"

"Hale told me."

"Sure."

"May I come in?" She wore a velvety navy jogging suit that hugged her every curve. Her hair was in one of those trademark ponytails of hers that usually started out neat and ended up in a mess—something he found phenomenally attractive. Par for the course, when he was around her, he wanted to touch her so badly that his fingertips itched.

Stepping aside, he let her enter.

"Nice," she said with a cautious smile.

How many times in the past few days had he imagined her here?

"Your view's amazing."

"Thanks." In the time they'd been apart, her voice had grown a shade more husky. Her complexion struck him as paler, too, instead of sun-kissed from the morning they'd spent fishing.

Hugging herself as if she were cold, she said, "It feels like you could just reach out and touch the arch."

"Yeah. Even as a kid, I was fascinated by it." Finally

remembering to close the door, he asked, "Can I get you anything? Coke? Beer?"

"No, thanks," she said with a faint smile and blowing him away with her subtle beauty. Had she always been this gorgeous? "Do you mind if we just talk?"

"That'd be great," he said, leading the way to a pair of soft red leather sofas that framed the view.

He waited for her to perch on one, then he took the other.

Just being near her sent his pulse haywire. His thought process clicked into gear. In an instant he knew he'd been a fool.

All along, he'd been an overemotional oaf. Tess might've done a number on him once, but not anymore. It was high time he took a turn behind his own wheel.

She licked her lips, sucked in a gallon of air. "I'm sure you're wondering what we could possibly say to each other, but—"

"Let me," he said.

"Okay."

"You can't imagine how sick I am for reacting the way I did at the inn. I was wrong. Damned wrong. And I'm sorry."

Her wavering smile didn't quite reach her eyes. In an instant telling him volumes about how she really felt.

"Why'd you even come?" he asked.

"What do you mean?"

"Isn't it obvious?" He laughed. "I'd hoped you were here because you saw something we shared worth salvaging, but—"

"Of course I do," she said, angling on the sofa to face him. "That's why—"

"No," he said, palms out to make the universal sign indicating stop. "I know this is going to sound awfully convenient, but before you showed up I was seriously contemplating calling Sadie to ask where I could find you. But seeing you now, I feel like we're strangers. It's as if every shred of chemistry we shared is gone."

"You're wrong, Heath. In fact, I was just thinking how…"

Ding-dong.

Arching his head back and closing his eyes, Heath couldn't imagine his twin having picked a worse time to visit.

"Expecting company?" Sadie asked.

"No," he said, the muscles in his jaw popping as he headed for the door, planning on telling Hale to get lost.

He opened the door, and sure enough there was his twin, hunched over and breathing heavily. "Bro… I'm so glad I found you, man. Listen, we've got to go."

"What're you talking about?" Heath asked. Why? *Why* couldn't Hale have picked any other afternoon—any other *moment*—to crash this private party? "Sarah's inside. Trust me, it's you who's got to go."

"Hale?" Sadie asked, meeting him at the door. "You seem upset. Something wrong?"

Heath wrinkled his forehead. What was up with Sarah's bizarre expressions? Eyes twitching and winking. Lips pursing and puckering. A glance at his brother showed him doing the same.

"Uh, *Sarah,*" his twin said with a suddenly jovial chuckle, "I hate to interrupt your meeting, but Heath and I have urgent business to hash over."

"What business?" Heath said, damn near close to

slamming the door in Hale's face. "Just a minute ago you said we had to go."

"Right. *Go* do business. I've gotta get you to sign stuff for me, man."

"What stuff?"

"A will?" Sadie suggested.

"Yes—a will. Thank you." Chuckling, he mocked himself with a conk to his forehead. "It's been a long day."

"In that case," she said, grabbing her purse from a chrome-and-glass table, "I'll leave you to—"

In the hall, the elevator chimed and the doors swished open.

"Crap," Hale said under his breath.

"Heath?" a woman who sounded suspiciously like Sarah said. "I called and called for you in the lobby, but you took off up the stairs before I could—" Upon seeing the trio gathered at Heath's open door, she froze.

Heath glanced over his shoulder at the woman to whom he'd been pouring his heart out just moments earlier. "Just a wild guess here, but I'm thinking the reason you and I felt no chemistry is because you and I, *Sadie*, have never officially met?"

She started to say something and then clamped her lips tight.

"Hale," Heath asked, "are you the spokesperson for this thankfully busted mission?"

"I'm not believing this," the genuine Sarah said—unless she was actually a triplet and hadn't yet gotten around to telling him. "So then your apology this afternoon at my office wasn't real?"

"What apology?" Heath demanded.

"Um, Sadie," Hale said, "wanna come help sign those papers?" He was already in the open elevator, furiously jabbing a button.

"Absolutely." She hustled past Heath, skimmed her hand along Sarah's shoulder and left, jogging into the elevator alongside Hale just as the doors swished shut.

"CAN YOU BELIEVE THOSE two?" Sarah said, flopping her hands at her side. "I'm sure Sadie's the ringleader. She controls every inch of her world at the inn. Guess all that power's gone to her head, and she now thinks her circle of influence includes me."

"Here I was guessing Hale was in charge. He's a fixer. Lose a race? Drive faster. Bored with your job? Get another one. Hell, if you're too busy to work, call your sap twin brother—he'll stand in for you."

"Add that onto my speech about Sadie," Sarah said with a sad snort. "Those two are so alike *they* should've been the twins."

"Where are my manners?" Heath said. "Come in."

Reflexively she shook her head. "I—I'm not sure why I'm even here."

"Without sounding egotistical, presumably to see me?"

Despite her best efforts to hold it together, she cracked a grin. "You got me there."

"How'd you know where I live?"

"You told me," she said, brushing past him to enter a space so grand that it nearly stole her breath. "Wow," she said, hands over her mouth, feeling as if she'd stepped into a church. "The view…it's everything you said and more."

I've got a penthouse with floor-to-ceiling windows and a view of the whole world. One of these days I want to explore you there—every inch of you. I want to erase every trace of heartache Greg put you through. With the tickling that'd followed, he had made her forget her ex—along with her every other problem.

Hit hard by the memory of not just kissing the man but of tickling, wrestling and *living* alongside him, Sarah had to force herself to breathe. How could he not remember saying those beautiful things? How could she have been so wrong in her assessment of his character?

She stood close to the window wall overlooking the Gateway Arch. She never should've come here. "I'm sorry," she said. "I'm just going to go. After our talk this afternoon—or I guess that would be my talk with your twin—I…"

Heath stood behind her, so close that his radiated heat seared her from head to heel. Her nerves were on fire. How could her body feel so electrified yet her heart so dull?

"Just so you know," he said softly, "I remember. We were horsing around. Kissing. Right after we'd damn near made love. That's when I told you about my view."

Something deep inside her released. He remembered. And the part of her that had been wounded over the notion he'd forgotten such a special moment was soothed. But then the crux of their problems wasn't about physical chemistry. That'd always worked between them. The issue here was that he didn't trust her. And that she doubted her innate lightning-quick trust of him.

"For the record," he said, close enough for his warm breath to brush the nape of her neck, "none of what I went through with Tess hurt half as bad as what went down between us." Curving his fingers around her shoulders, he said, "I'm sorry, Sarah. So damned sorry. The way I behaved was unforgivable. When I thought you and that Neanderthal hunk were an item, I was out of my mind with jealousy. The thought of that man touching you…kissing you…it was too much. I snapped. I'm sorry. So—"

"Stop," she said, turning to press her cheek against that wall of his chest that she'd so grown to love. But was love enough? Weren't they both still, in a sense, damaged goods? "As for this weekend, I'm sorry, too. The whole thing was a start-to-finish disaster."

"Even meeting me?"

Judging by how miserable I've been, meeting you was quite possibly the biggest mess of all.

Hugging him with freshened fervor, she denied the hateful thought. It scared her how hard and fast she'd fallen for the man. How could she feel as if she'd known him forever yet didn't really know him at all? It didn't make sense. *Couldn't* make sense. She didn't need this complication in her life.

Yet pressing against him made her quiver with need. Suddenly she was tired of talk and ready for action. Ludicrous, but there it was. Being in the same room with him was the equivalent to landing a sumptuous dessert buffet in the middle of a Weight Watchers meeting!

"Sarah?" Easing her back, he tipped up her chin, forcing her gaze to meet his. "Do you think meeting me was a mistake?"

Throat aching, she said, "I don't know what to think. Being with you again, I can't get past this craving to just devour you. Which is wrong but—"

He silenced her with a kiss so elemental and raw that her heart thundered and her legs refused to hold her weight. Which didn't matter, seeing how she was falling and he was falling and in a fevered tangle they ended up on the thickly carpeted floor with him on top.

A few minutes later, her breath ragged, she said, "Th-this is crazy. The way, whenever I'm around you, I lose all sense of control."

"Ditto."

"So what do you want to do?"

"Truth?" As usual, his sexy grin stole what little remained of her breath.

Unable to speak, she nodded.

"Do something equally out of control—like run off to Vegas and marry you, then keep you in my arms for the rest of our lives."

"Sounds great," Sarah said, pulse racing. "But Sadie's got her heart set on a double Christmas wedding."

"Assuming you'd even consider giving her what she wants, does that mean you've forgiven me for pulling the twin switch?"

"If you forgive me. It really *is* kinda funny, if you think about it."

"Yeah, only I'm not going to laugh till I have something of mine around you, binding you to me."

"Sounds doable," she said, slipping her arms around his waist, pressing her cheek to his deliciously solid chest. "How about sealing our deal with a hug?"

"Mmm…no good. Should be something more

substantial. Jewelry. For you—" kiss, kiss "—pricey jewelry."

"I like the sound of that." Pushing free of him, she said, "And I think I have just the right thing."

"What're you doing?" he asked while she dashed off to grab her purse.

"You'll see." Seconds later she withdrew a crumpled white bag.

"Is that what I think it is?" he asked, eyebrows raised. "I figured you'd thrown it in the lake for swan food."

"Never," she said, holding the bag and its contents to her heart. "The necklace and earrings are beautiful, but they don't compare to the beauty of the sentiment behind your giving them to me. I love you, *Heath*."

"I love you, *Sarah*."

Handing him the bag, then turning her back to him and raising her hair, she asked, "Would you please put them on for me? I couldn't bear the thought of wearing these without you."

"It'd be my pleasure," he said, fulfilling her fantasy of the moment by brushing the backs of his warm, strong fingers along her neck, then pressing a tingle-inducing kiss behind her right ear. Giving her a gentle spin, he surveyed his handiwork against the backdrop of the open vee of her blouse. "Gorgeous. Just like you."

"Nope," she said with a firm shake of her head. "Like you."

"You."

"No, you."

"Woman," he said, scooping her into his arms, then hushing her with a kiss, "are we going to stand here arguing or are we finally going to get around to making love?"

"Seeing how I'm no longer standing, I'd say let's skip the bickering and go straight to love."

After thoroughly kissing her again, he said, "I couldn't agree more."

* * * * *

Set in darkness beyond the ordinary world.
Passionate tales of life and death.
With characters' lives ruled by laws the
everyday world can't begin to imagine.

n●cturne

It's time to discover the Raintree trilogy...

New York Times bestselling author
LINDA HOWARD
brings you the dramatic first book
RAINTREE: INFERNO

The Ansara Wizards are rising and the Raintree clan
must rejoin the battle against their foes, testing their
powers, relationships and forcing upon them lives
they never could have imagined before...

Turn the page for a sneak preview
of the captivating first book
in the Raintree trilogy,
RAINTREE: INFERNO
by LINDA HOWARD
On sale April.

Dante Raintree stood with his arms crossed as he watched the woman on the monitor. The image was in black and white to better show details; color distracted the brain. He focused on her hands, watching every move she made, but what struck him most was how uncommonly *still* she was. She didn't fidget or play with her chips, or look around at the other players. She peeked once at her down card, then didn't touch it again, signaling for another hit by tapping a fingernail on the table. Just because she didn't seem to be paying attention to the other players, though, didn't mean she was as unaware as she seemed.

"What's her name?" Dante asked.

"Lorna Clay," replied his chief of security, Al Rayburn.

"At first I thought she was counting, but she doesn't pay enough attention."

"She's paying attention, all right," Dante murmured. "You just don't see her doing it." A card counter had to remember every card played. Supposedly counting cards was impossible with the number of decks used by the casinos, but there were those rare individuals who could calculate the odds even with multiple decks.

"I thought that, too," said Al. "But look at this piece of tape coming up. Someone she knows comes up to her and speaks, she looks around and starts chatting, completely misses the play of the people to her left— and doesn't look around even when the deal comes back to her, just taps that finger. And damn if she didn't win. Again."

Dante watched the tape, rewound it, watched it again. Then he watched it a third time. There had to be something he was missing, because he couldn't pick out a single giveaway.

"If she's cheating," Al said with something like respect, "she's the best I've ever seen."

"What does your gut say?"

Al scratched the side of his jaw, considering. Finally, he said, "If she isn't cheating, she's the luckiest person walking. She wins. Week in, week out, she wins. Never a huge amount, but I ran the numbers and she's into us for about five grand a week. Hell, boss, on her way out of the casino she'll stop by a slot machine, feed a dollar in and walk away with at least fifty. It's never the same machine, either. I've had her watched, I've had her followed, I've even looked for the same faces in the casino every time she's in here, and I can't find a common denominator."

"Is she here now?"

"She came in about half an hour ago. She's playing blackjack, as usual."

"Bring her to my office," Dante said, making a swift decision. "Don't make a scene."

"Got it," said Al, turning on his heel and leaving the security center.

Dante left, too, going up to his office. His face was calm. Normally he would leave it to Al to deal with a cheater, but he was curious. How was she doing it? There were a lot of bad cheaters, a few good ones, and every so often one would come along who was the stuff of which legends were made: the cheater who didn't get caught, even when people were alert and the camera was on him—or, in this case, her.

It was possible to simply be lucky, as most people understood luck. Chance could turn a habitual loser into a big-time winner. Casinos, in fact, thrived on that hope. But luck itself wasn't habitual, and he knew that what passed for luck was often something else: cheating. And there was the other kind of luck, the kind he himself possessed, but it depended not on chance but on who and what he was. He knew it was an innate power and not Dame Fortune's erratic smile. Since power like his was rare, the odds made it likely the woman he'd been watching was merely a very clever cheat.

Her skill could provide her with a very good living, he thought, doing some swift calculations in his head. Five grand a week equaled $260,000 a year, and that was just from his casino. She probably hit them all, careful to keep the numbers relatively low so she stayed under the radar.

He wondered how long she'd been taking him, how long she'd been winning a little here, a little there, before Al noticed.

The curtains were open on the wall-to-wall window

in his office, giving the impression, when one first opened the door, of stepping out onto a covered balcony. The glazed window faced·west, so he could catch the sunsets. The sun was low now, the sky painted in purple and gold. At his home in the mountains, most of the windows faced east, affording him views of the sunrise. Something in him needed both the greeting and the goodbye of the sun. He'd always been drawn to sunlight, maybe because fire was his element to call, to control.

He checked his internal time: four minutes until sundown. Without checking the sunrise tables every day, he knew exactly when the sun would slide behind the mountains. He didn't own an alarm clock. He didn't need one. He was so acutely attuned to the sun's position that he had only to check within himself to know the time. As for waking at a particular time, he was one of those people who could tell himself to wake at a certain time, and he did. That talent had nothing to do with being Raintree, so he didn't have to hide it; a lot of perfectly ordinary people had the same ability.

He had other talents and abilities, however, that did require careful shielding. The long days of summer instilled in him an almost sexual high, when he could feel contained power buzzing just beneath his skin. He had to be doubly careful not to cause candles to leap into flame just by his presence, or to start wildfires with a glance in the dry-as-tinder brush. He loved Reno; he didn't want to burn it down. He just felt so damn *alive* with all the sunshine pouring down that he wanted to let the energy pour through him instead of holding it inside.

This must be how his brother Gideon felt while pulling lightning, all that hot power searing through his muscles, his veins. They had this in common, the connection with raw power. All the members of the far-flung Raintree clan had some power, some heightened ability, but only members of the royal family could channel and control the earth's natural energies.

Dante wasn't just of the royal family, he was the Dranir, the leader of the entire clan. "Dranir" was synonymous with king, but the position he held wasn't ceremonial, it was one of sheer power. He was the oldest son of the previous Dranir, but he would have been passed over for the position if he hadn't also inherited the power to hold it.

Behind him came Al's distinctive knock on the door. The outer office was empty, Dante's secretary having gone home hours before. "Come in," he called, not turning from his view of the sunset.

The door opened, and Al said, "Mr. Raintree, this is Lorna Clay."

Dante turned and looked at the woman, all his senses on alert. The first thing he noticed was the vibrant color of her hair, a rich, dark red that encompassed a multitude of shades from copper to burgundy. The warm amber light danced along the iridescent strands, and he felt a hard tug of sheer lust in his gut. Looking at her hair was almost like looking at fire, and he had the same reaction.

The second thing he noticed was that she was spitting mad.

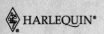

Mediterranean NIGHTS™

Tycoon Elias Stamos is launching his newest luxury cruise ship from his home port in Greece. But someone from his past is eager to expose old secrets and to see the Stamos empire crumble.

Mediterranean Nights
launches in June 2007 with...

Love can be the most *foreign language*

Ingrid Weaver

FROM RUSSIA, WITH LOVE

FROM RUSSIA, WITH LOVE
by *Ingrid Weaver*

Join the guests and crew of *Alexandra's Dream* as they are drawn into a world of glamour, romance and intrigue in this new 12-book series.

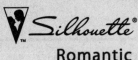

Romantic
SUSPENSE

Sparked *by Danger,*
Fueled *by Passion.*

*This month and every month look for
four new heart-racing romances
set against a backdrop of suspense!*

Available in May 2007

Safety in Numbers
(Wild West Bodyguards miniseries)
by **Carla Cassidy**

Jackson's Woman
by **Maggie Price**

Shadow Warrior
(Night Guardians miniseries)
by **Linda Conrad**

One Cool Lawman
by **Diane Pershing**

Available wherever you buy books!

Visit Silhouette Books at www.eHarlequin.com   SRS0407

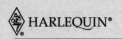

HARLEQUIN®

American ROMANCE®

A THREE-BOOK SERIES BY BELOVED AUTHOR

Judy Christenberry

Dallas Duets

What's behind the doors of
the Yellow Rose Lane apartments?
Love, Texas-style!

THE MARRYING KIND
May 2007

Jonathan Davis was many things—a millionaire,
a player, a catch. But he'd never be a husband.
For him, "marriage" equaled "mistake." Diane Black
was a forever kind of woman, a babies-and-minivan
kind of woman. But John was confident he could
date her and still avoid that trap.
Until he kissed her…

Also watch for:
DADDY NEXT DOOR
January 2007

MOMMY FOR A MINUTE
August 2007

Available wherever Harlequin books are sold.